I0788706

HEART
OF
SHADOW

OTHER SERIES BY SARAH K. L. WILSON

DRAGON SCHOOL

DRAGON CHAMELEON

DRAGON TIDE

BRIDGE OF LEGENDS

TANGLED FAE

EMPIRE OF WAR & WINGS

PHOENIX HEART

BLUEBEARD'S SECRET

Heart of Shadow

Seven Swords
Book 1

Sarah K. L. Wilson

Published by Sparkflight Books, 2021

This is a work of fiction. Similarities to real people, places, or events are entirely coincidental.

HEART OF SHADOW
First Edition. November 24, 2021
Copyright © 2021 Sarah K. L. Wilson
ISBN : 978-1-990516-01-6
Cover Art by Mandy Jurgens
Written by Sarah K. L. Wilson
Published by Sparkflight Books
www.sarahklwilson.com

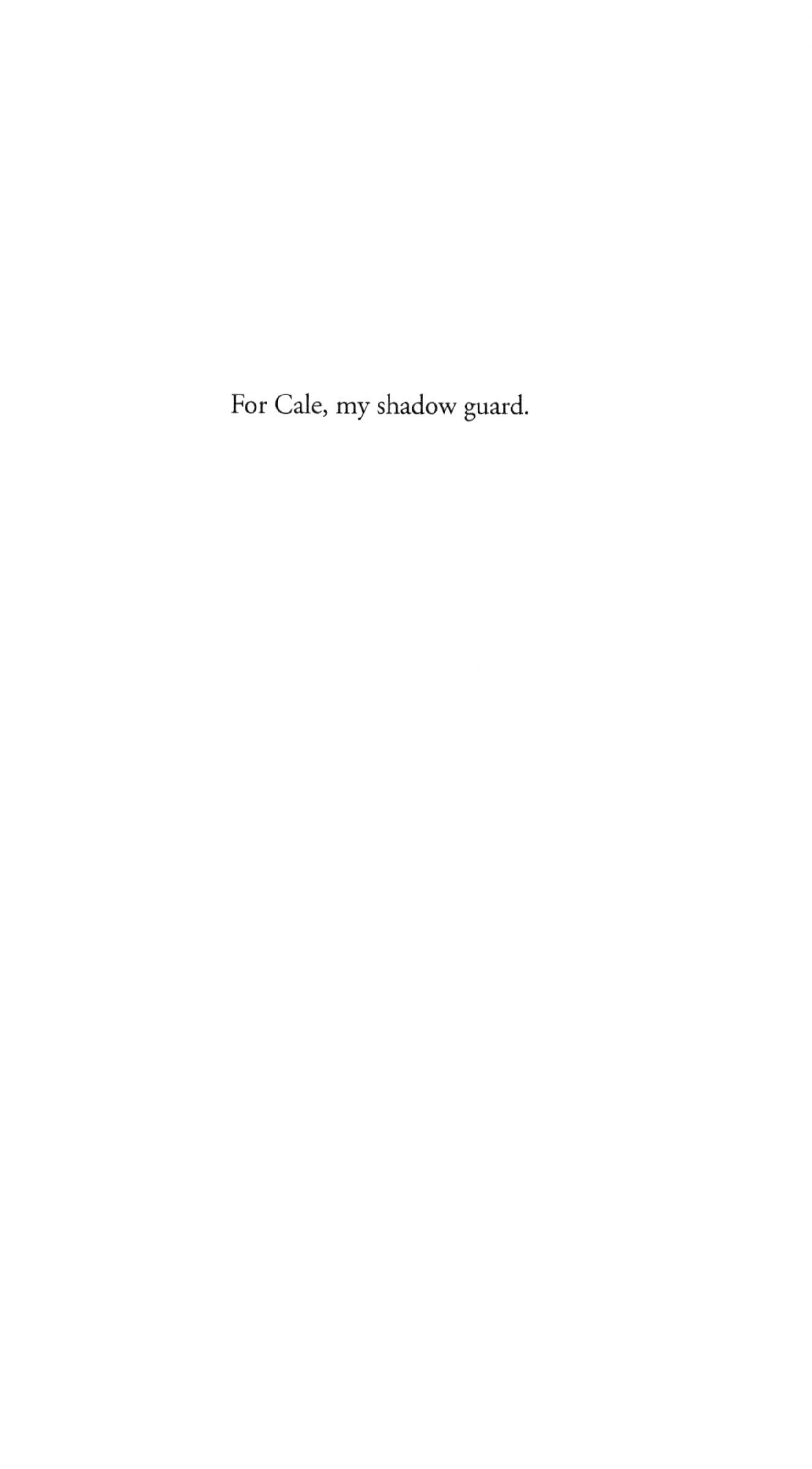

For Cale, my shadow guard.

Chapter One

I'm shattering, shattering, shattering. My fingers are icicles smashing to fragments. Every breath is shards of glass slicing through my lungs.

He's in the room outside my closet door looking under the bed and opening drawers. And I still haven't opened the box. I've been working on this lock with a letter opener and a bit of twisted metal for a day and a half. My fingers are nicked and bloody and they hurt all the time.

I almost had it a few hours ago, but then my hand shook, and the last tumbler fell back, and I lost every bit of progress. An itch is forming between my shoulder blades from nervous sweat, and my bottom lip is trembling so hard, and I can't make it stop because this time, if I don't get the box open, I'm definitely going to die instead of just maybe.

Because he is right outside my door.

And he's hunting me.

Just a few days ago he was the cook's boy. He brought in firewood and turned spits and joked with the guards when they came in the back to tease cook into giving them hot buns and tea. One day he gave me a daisy with my morning breakfast, his brown eyes shy in a face still soft with youth.

"Because it's smiling like you," had been his stumbling explanation and now he's outside my door smashing the wardrobe to splinters because I'm not inside it.

And oh skies, I'm not going to get this lock open. I'm going to fail again. And then all I'll have to fight him will be my grandfather's letter opener. He used it to hold off a pack of goblins intent on eating his flesh – or at least that's the story he told me when I was small. But this is no pack of goblins, and I am not grandfather.

I am Isaletta.

I drank clover tea on my eighteenth birthday, five days ago. I want to be a famous cartographer someday. I am the daughter of Admiral Redtide.

I will be dead if I don't get this lock open.

That's the fourth tumbler turning. I've been this far now at least a dozen times but there's a fifth tumbler and maybe more – oh sweet depths, I hope there isn't more! I ease my pick into the little dip between them and try for what feels like the hundred thousandth time to find the leverage I need to shift that last tumbler. The vibrations in the little pick tell me that I've caught the edge of something.

Crash.

Something new has broken on the other side of the door. The closet handle jiggles. It's always been loose and the metal jingles when you try to open it while it's locked.

Blood fills my mouth. I've bitten my tongue.

Please. If there is a divine sovereign out there, hear my prayer and let this last tumbler turn.

The handle jingles again and his harsh breathing gusts so loudly that I can hear it through two inches of oak door.

My cheeks are hot with streaming tears, but I must not make a sound. I haven't made a sound in four days. Except for the tiny scratching sound of trying to pick this lock.

I know what is coming and I know I can't afford to flinch. He'll try to bash the door down. He won't be the first.

It was the footman the first day. But he was already weak, and he had no weapon. His fists were not enough to shatter oak. I don't think that the cook's boy is only using his fists. But I know that whatever he does, I must not jump or flinch and lose my place in the tumblers.

The closet shudders, but I hold my breath and keep my hands still. The air in my lungs saws through my chest painfully, but silently. I have become practiced at silence just like I am practiced at listening to the constant drip of the rain and schooled in remaining still in the ever-present darkness of the closet.

Another bang from the room suggests that the cook's boy is putting his shoulder into his work. The dust on the floor bounces when he flings himself at the door again. My bits of metal are getting slippery. I'm sweating in ways I can't stop and can't allow.

I need this box open. I need what is in it. And oh, divine sovereign, don't let my father have lied to me about this box.

I feel the tumbler ease just a little and I can't quite hold back my excited gasp.

"You're in there, poppet. I know you are."

That's not Herralt's voice. I know his voice. It's unsteady as he eases into manhood. But it does not wheedle like that.

I can't afford to move too fast and lose my pressure on the tumbler. I try to think of anything except the boy breaking down the door.

Out there, far to the south, my father sails with his fleet bearing Lord and Lady Harrowcross to the Poco Pera Islands where they will drink vanilla rum and bathe their feet in the warm turquoise seas and dream as the susurrating songs of the Poco people and even if I fail here, he will never know how I lived my last days.

I cling to that. And I take a deep breath and twist.

Light pours into the closet through a narrow sliver as the wood of the door splinters with a crack. He found an axe.

But my hands have not shaken too badly. I have not lost my purchase. I squeeze my eyes shut and channel all my focus into my fingers and seeing the tumblers in my head and I *twist*.

The axe is buried deep. He's wrenching it back and forth to free it. Oak does not break easily and neither do I.

The last tumbler shifts, and the lock opens with a snick at the same moment that all his efforts break the lock of my door. He wrenches it open as I pry up the lid.

Breath gusts from my lungs but this is not shock, it's relief. My father didn't lie. My salvation gleams in the bright light pouring into the closet.

My hands fit around the grip of the sword as if it was made for them. It's balanced and easy to lift – which is good because I have only a heartbeat to draw it from the velvet bed it lies on and lift it in front of me like a horn before he crashes through the door, arms raised, axe over his head.

Not like that. Hold it higher. Slide your bottom hand lower. Have you never held a sword before?

The thoughts aren't mine but they're useful. I adjust as Herrault roars toward me.

He doesn't look surprised as the sharp blade slides through his belly.

I can't stop the shake in my hands, though. I can't stop the way my breath gulps.

Steady now! This is no tea ceremony. It's killing. The steadier you are, the faster it's done.

He stumbles back and comes off my blade, one hand clutching his belly, the other raising his axe. His mouth opens and I'm braced for his roar, but it doesn't come. Instead, something that looks like pink smoke rolls out of his mouth and coalesces into a creature with holes for eyes and a screaming mouth. Its talons rip through the air as it claws toward me.

I bite back my scream.

Out of the closet! Out! No room to maneuver in here!

I stumble out, but more room isn't going to help me. I'm no swordswoman. I should flee while I can.

You can't. He'll hack that axe into your soft back. Keep the blade up. Higher. Hold this stance.

Herrault's mouth twists and he lunges toward me, axe raised as the strange smoke creature screeches, darting forward just inches from my face.

I don't scream. I just freeze like a rabbit faced with a slathering dog. The light pouring through the window behind me casts my shadow over his face and I can't see his expression anymore.

And then darkness grips the pink smoke, and it rips into a thousand tiny scraps and dissipates.

Now I scream. It starts as a squeak and builds into a thready wail.

And something shifts.

I don't know what I'm seeing. I'm probably hallucinating. The first few days that I was locked in the closet, I hallucinated all kinds of things. I thought I heard friends. Saviors. Thought I could smell bread baking.

Now, I'm seeing a dark shadow coalesce and then lunge. It lifts Herrault up and before he can scream, it throws him, and I brace myself as he falls with his neck directly on my blade. It's so sharp that it slices through flesh without knocking me over from the force. I'm left gasping, shocked and horrified as I try to keep my balance.

I'm going to be sick.

There is no shadow now, just a bloody sword in my hands and a dead boy at my feet and I'm going to vomit.

I turn to the side and heave, but I haven't eaten in almost two days, and nothing comes up but a thready stream of acid and water.

I'm no swordswoman. I'm no guard. I don't even spend time in the courtyard when they're killing chickens. I avoid looking at what I've done as I clean the blade with numb hands on the hanging tapestry there. It's a tapestry of Veronika, the warrior angel who slew an army to save a besieged city. In the woven threads she's shown on a white horse with three squalling babes in her arms. I have saved no one but myself, and still, I think she wouldn't mind that I'm wiping life's blood onto her tapestry.

It can't be real. Pink smoke. Shadows fighting my battles for me. None of this can be real.

The shake in my hands has trembled up my arms and I'm fully in its grip now.

But you know to clean the blade. You know to show it respect. I can work with that.

The blade sparkles in my hand – dark as night, even the wrapped hilt, even the gems on the pommel.

"What's in the box," I had asked my father when I was small. He kept it always on a high shelf in his study – free of dust, polished, and shining in the sun as only lacquer does.

"An ancient evil and a tale."

"How can evil be in a box?" I had asked, wide-eyed as he drew me onto his lap, balanced me there, and put my hands on the hilt of his sword.

"All swords are evil, Ilsaletta," he said gently. "For they are made for one thing only – to slice the cord of a man's life. But some evils are necessary or there will be no good."

"Is there a sword in the box?" I had asked.

He tucked a strand of hair behind my ear tenderly and smiled. "So, they say. I have never opened the box and I never will. The key was lost long before my time and I am too old to be a fool. What is locked up is often best kept that way. This sword is more than a tool. It's possessed by an ancient evil with a heart of its own. A dark, shadow heart. Only a fool would want to loose that upon the world."

Coward's words. They fear me. They wish they had my great power.

Only the insane hear voices in their heads and since I am hearing a voice, I must be mad.

You are not mad.

If I am not mad, then why am I standing over a dead boy with shaking hands and a dark blade, listening to a baritone voice talk in my head?

And what a voice. It is thick and deep like the keel of a ship plunging into the waves and there's a burr to it, like a slight fray in the bow of a violin. It shivers up my spine and down again, playing me like I am the instrument and it is the musician.

You hear a baritone voice because a creature with a baritone voice is talking in your head.

Creature?

You saw me. I was the shadow that aided your efforts to slay the corricle.

What's a corricle?

The vessel of an evil being. The kind of being I usually try to avoid – or slay, as the mood takes me.

Like the sword I held in my trembling hands. The sword that I should put back in the box.

No! Definitely don't do that.

I hesitate. I haven't talked to someone else in four days. My mind aches for company.

If you lock the sword away, how will you defend yourself if more of them come? Be reasonable.

I'm already shivering, so there's no new reaction to his thoughts, but I know he's right. I watched from the study window that first night.

Arnault, the captain of the guard slew the first to attack him. When the creature fell it was like a ringing bell and a dozen more poured in from every direction. They overwhelmed him and dragged him under the mass of their bodies. And that was when I locked myself in the closet.

Dark memories, mortal girl. Dark, dark musings.

I am not a dark person. I see sunshine in between clouds. I notice the flower sprouting, not the crumbling wall under it. I save the goats born with deformities.

Even the brightest of lights must face the shadow someday. Today, is your day. But you are fortunate. I am with you.

Scuffling sounds meet my ears from somewhere below. I freeze. Those sounds are too large to be rats.

More enemies. Wait for them …

I bite my lip and ease slowly back toward the closet. There has been safety there before.

With a fresh kill in front of the door, you will tell the whole world where you came from. Better to stand firm and face them as they come. Cowardice is the friend of fools.

I am not firm. I am shattering. I am pieces of the girl I once was.

Not true. It only feels like that for now. A first kill will do that. In time, your pieces will weld back together – stronger in the places where they broke.

Who are you?

I close the door of the closet behind me and turn the key in the lock, alone in the dark once more except for the ray of light shining through the hole the axe cut.

I am a Nakuraki. Guardian of empires, defender of queens, caught in the shadow of this dark sword for a thousand years. And released now in your time of need.

That is impossible. People don't live in the shadows of swords.

I am not a person – not anymore. Have you heard of the boogeyman?

The butler liked to tell scary stories when he was deep in his cups and one was of the boogeyman who lived in closets and under the bed. Light a candle and he fled.

I'm like that. But I don't live under the bed. I live in a shadow.

How did you get in the sword's shadow?

I cannot say. Long have I slumbered, untouched. I have lost much. My memories are moth-eaten and they crumble to dust in my hands.

I worry my lip between my teeth. I should put the sword back in the box. If it is really haunted by some kind of boogeyman, then it is no wonder that my father has kept it locked up. No wonder he has pronounced it evil.

But my hands feel heavy at the thought of locking it back in the box. It is my only weapon. And in my closet sanctuary, I am low on water. By tomorrow I will have nothing to drink. I haven't had food in two days.

But worse than all of it is the loneliness and fear. Every

moment drags on and on. Every bump in the great house forces my heart to spike with fear and there is no one to help me be brave. There is no one to bear it all with me.

The Nakuraki bears the danger for the Vali. The Nakuraki is the companion of the right hand and the guide to the foot.

I don't know what any of that means.

It means I will be here with you – if you will trust me. I will speak the vows of the Nakuraki to you – vows that will protect you and bind me in your service. Vows that will keep you safe.

Footsteps. They are clear even with the Nakuraki speaking in my mind. Someone is coming and there are no friends left in my father's great house. The guards are dead or turned. Cook and the maids and my father's manager and now even the kitchen boy – are all dead or dying.

Whoever is still here will want me dead, too.

I know my limits. Without the Nakuraki's help, Herrault would have split my head with that axe.

I swallow down the fear climbing up my throat. I need to make a decision. I am weak and small and untrained for this. My skill with maps and languages is nothing in a world of kill or be killed. My best hope is a powerful ally and the only one offering that to me is the Nakuraki.

But if I accept his help, what will happen to me? Will he take me over like the smoke took over Herrault?

That is not my way. Even shattered as I am, I have not lost my honor.

Will I die, unable to bear his essence – just like the guard I saw in the courtyard below who had doubled over, screaming about a voice and then clutched his throat and died on the spot?

I will die before I allow that.

Are you not dead?

His baritone laughter in my mind is not comforting at all.

The door of my father's study creaks open and heavy breathing tells me the newcomer is in a hurry.

I must decide right now, or it will be too late.

I protected Queen Gersa of Felinor from the raving priests of the Thunder God. I slew two hundred that day.

Where was Felinor and who was Queen Gersa?

I ... he sounds confused. *I can't remember.*

But it is still the best offer available to me.

I agree, Nakuraki. I wish to bind you in my service.

I am worried by the glee I feel in his mental voice. *Let it be done!*

Nakuraki

I am born again. Reiterated. Made new.

I feel the thrill of life pouring through me as the sword makes a shadow again and I taste fear and desperation in the soul nearest me. There is violence to be had and it is close by.

My memories are shreds and tatters. I reach for them and they're gone but I know enough to guide these novice hands and feet into the forms of the sword.

A little lower, I nudge her.

And to my eyes, she is bright as the sun, a goddess born before me. Her big eyes and trembling lips are wide as if she might drop blessings on my head right now and her dark skin and darker hair are lit with the light of glory.

I have never met a goddess before – not even a newly-made one. I hardly know what to say. I ought to make obeisance to her.

Danger. She's in danger. Someone batters at her door.

And I am the black darkness of judgment and silky rage and it matters not that I am only minutes old. It matters not that I am guided by nothing but scraps of other men's memories. It matters only that she is safe, that she lives. This goddess needs a defender.

I can live a whole life in the time I spend keeping her safe.

CHAPTER TWO

I've never taken a vow of any kind and my skin tingles as I silently kneel at his prompting. Shouldn't the person taking the vow kneel?

We both must. Close your eyes.

His voice is rumbly where it dips as he speaks inside my mind. I imagine it sounds like a bear must – dark and deep and on the edge of violence. I should feel invaded by how he is in my thoughts, but I feel only warm and slightly tingly.

The floor outside creaks and my legs are jelly, wobbling so badly that I'm afraid the intruder will hear. I'm snapped back to the present. I don't want to close my eyes. What if that is the moment the closet doors open?

I grip the hilt of the black sword in my sweating palms, tip pressed into the closet floor.

Trust me.

I close my eyes. Something tingles on my forehead and the tip of my nose.

Keep them closed. I kneel before you and press my forehead and nose to yours. This is the beginning of our binding. It will not be completed until two mornings hence.

I didn't have three days to kneel here with my eyes shut.

Nor will you. Now, stay still for just a moment and hear the words of my vow. He sounded nervous now. Uncertain. What does it take to make a sword-spirit uncertain? *I, Vargaard of the Spineheights, make this soul vow. In your shadow may I dwell that your shadow I may be. Your sorrows I will borrow, your pain I will bear, the lifting of your head shall be my glory, and the light of your eyes my delight. To the last drop of my blood, I will defend you, screaming defiance into the depths.* He pauses here as if he is overcome by some emotion and then he continues. *If I fail in my vow, may curses fall on my head, and may my soul walk the howling roads beyond the veil.*

My teeth rattle so hard that I'm worried I'm going to be heard and my eyes fly open just in time to see shadow dissipating from right before my face. Had we truly been nose to nose? He is made of shadow – insubstantial and impossible to touch – and yet I feel touched by him.

I feel like I should repay vow for vow and yet I do not know how.

No return is required. This is not a bargain – unless it is a bargain I make with myself.

Clumsily, I reach one hand down and nick my finger on the blade of my sword and spatter the blood on the ground. I've seen my father do this when making bargains. It's only right that I give something, too.

"This blood tells you that I will deal fairly with you," I whisper. "That I will treat you with the value of my own blood."

I've never made a vow before and mine feels clumsy and

childish next to his.

You honor me too much. His mental voice sounds breathless.

The doorknob rattles. Again.

And my belly constricts with fear. I must not make a sound.

Oh no, mortal girl. No sound is needed. Brace yourself for battle.

The door is wrenched open and I'm on my feet in a flash, my black blade raised. I know enough to get the tip up, even if I know nothing of the hard life of wielding this blade.

Before me is Havestock – my father's clerk. Or what was once Havestock. He twists his hands around one of the guard's swords, his eyes wild.

"Come out, Ilsaletta." His voice is all wrong. "How have you survived the plague that has taken so many others? I have watched everyone else sicken and die and yet you've been hiding here, little dove. So quiet. So soft …"

My heart is in my throat. No one is safe who is calling me soft. Especially not when they carry a sword.

Fear not. Step forward – just one step and do it with care, keep your weight on the back foot. I like the name Ilsaletta – is that truly your name?

I take the step just the way he told me to, and my forward foot feels vulnerable.

"We'll go find your father, Ilsaletta," Havestock says in a high voice, his eyes flicking to poor Herrault and back. "No need for violence."

"Then why are you holding a sword?" My voice is raw from disuse and rough from the terrified tears I've cried silently and alone these past few days.

You will not be alone now. That much I can vow.

Havestock laughs. His laugh is high-pitched, and it doesn't show in his eyes. I grit my teeth together.

Take one more step out of the closet. I need the space.

For what? The words stutter in my mind.

I don't want to move. If I stay still, I will be safe. But no, I can be courageous – even if it feels right now like I can't be. I can take a step.

I take it slowly. My knees are still weak. I feel feverish – but that's just the fear filling me like a wineskin about to burst.

Havestock lunges forward so fast that I squeak like a mouse. I can't get my sword up. His hand grabs my throat. Thrashing isn't helping me, but I do it anyway.

Vargaard!

I like my name in your thoughts.

All I can see is Havestock's bloodshot eyes and the fleck of spittle on his lips. I'm going to die seeing this. I try to thrust with the sword, but he captures my other wrist in his, mashing the bones together. I try to scream. It comes out as a rasping gurgle.

Something reaches around me, and I can't see Havestock's face anymore. It goes dark in shadow. There's a crunch – a sickening snap – and the hand holding my throat drops me. I stumble backward, clutching my throat in my good hand, and pulling the injured one tightly against myself. My back hits a bookcase on the study wall and a book falls from the case. I don't even check to be sure it is not ruined. My stumble has snapped the shadow backward with me and now I see Havestock's body has been – folded – somehow. His arms and legs twist around him in unnatural ways as if he is a pair of stockings rolled up and ready to be put in a drawer.

My heart is hammering. Pain blossoms in my throat. My vision is darkening. I fight against what I know this is – my mind trying to shut down against the horror. I can't allow it. I must keep my feet.

We'll get better at that. His rumbling voice sounds embarrassed. *The first time is always tough. I remember that now.*

Better at what? Folding people? I'd be scoffing, but my throat is fire and agony. I'm going to be hysterical if I don't get a hold of myself.

Don't look at the body. Look somewhere else.

I spin. The bookshelf. The book I knocked off lies open on the floor and the feel of its pages soothes my fingers. Just glancing at the maps in it brings back memories of my father.

See? That's better. I'll be faster next time, and no one will touch you. I had forgotten that it takes time to find my form. I am new and with newness comes learning.

But he'd helped me just fine the first time.

That was before I was bound to you. I live in your shadow now.

A metaphor.

Perhaps. But it is also literal. I will dwell within the confines of your shadow, sword-bearer, and I may not leave it at any time. Though, if I am anchored to it, I can reach and stretch around you to repel your enemies. We will learn the limits of this together.

Hopefully, this wouldn't happen again. Hopefully, I could sneak out of the town and run for safety. Felgrast, perhaps. Or Mavenroe.

I grip the sword hilt in shaking hands as my eyes rove around the ruined library. Books and papers are scattered everywhere. Shelves are splintered and trinkets cast to the ground. It's a ruin. But I have the sword. And that means I have Vargaard.

Before we leave this place, we need to talk, Ilsaletta. His mind caresses my name like fine silk.

Tremors pass over me. I am in no mood to talk.

Tell me what has befallen your home and town.

All I can smell is death in the air. I clutch the bookcase, my eyes pinching shut.

Walk to the window. I will watch for us while you take in air.

I stumble to obey. It's good advice and I won't ignore it. I haven't had a breath of fresh air in days. I shove the shutters open and dull light spills over me. It's very cloudy outside. I will not have much of a shadow if I walk out there now.

You will still have a little shadow. There is always a little light.

And what about when there is no light?

I will cling so close I will cover you like a skim of oil protects water from the air.

Smoke drifts up into the air over the village in swirls and eddies. The ash in it is large flakes that float and drift – like black letters sent down from heaven. I have never liked the smell of smoke. To me, it always smells of danger.

Ice fills my veins as I look at the silent village. My father built his house on a high rock beside the sea, but the hamlet of Saltfast spreads below – a short walk from the great house, but close enough to see the town square. I cannot tell what I am seeing along the road or at the town center. Strange lumps lay still as if someone flung stones across the cobbles. There are gouges in the town – great black slashes made by fires that have burned out. From them, ashes float up into the sky. The rain must have put the fires out.

I take the breath Vargaard asked for and fill my lungs with something other than the stink of this room.

And now, if you please, your story.

CHAPTER THREE

Five days ago, I turned eighteen and that evening I was sitting here in my father's study, reading from his secret book that he thinks I don't know about and missing him. I could almost smell his fennel after-shave and as my fingers ran down the code in his book, I thought about the places he would sail to on his ship and the scents of spices at the docks and the salt of the sea in the breeze.

The upstairs maid had come up with a tray of food and tea for me and a huge pitcher of water for washing up.

"You're filthy all over!" she'd said with a click of her tongue.

I was not filthy, but I'd gone for a walk up the shore before I came home and I'll admit that I cried as I walked because I was missing my father and as much as I was missing him, I also feared his return because he said that when he came back, he would be bringing a husband for me. I do not want a husband and the thought had been weighing heavily on me.

Which was why I ignored the pitcher of wash water. Fortunately. And the tureen of hot biscuits under a lid, and the fruit, and the dried sausages.

I was so deep in my own glum mood that it wasn't until the

maid was nearly out of the room that I noticed she walked with a bit of a stumble.

"Are you injured, Betsy?" I asked and she stopped, surprised.

"Oh! No, just tired, Lady Ilsaletta."

But her face was pink and so I stood up and came around the desk and narrowed my eyes and asked, "Why are you lying to me?"

"Oh, lady!" she gasped. "Please don't tell Mistress Andza on me! I went into the village to visit my sister and there's sickness there and perhaps I've caught it."

"Sickness?" I pressed.

"It had only just come. A boy at the inn had a fever and one of the stable hands, but no one would say more because they were too excited by the news."

"What news?" I asked because what kind of news was more exciting than sickness in the town?

"A brace of lords and a half dozen soldiers came to the inn just an hour before I arrived, Lady Ilsaletta. And a fine lady with them – a lady finer than you, if you'll forgive me."

I waved that comment aside. What did I care if a lady was finer than me? There were plenty of ladies finer than me and likely plenty of women. I spent most of my time poring over my father's books, learning trade routes and languages and reading about history and court politics and theories of the court philosophers. Since my father had many books and not much in the way of necklaces or dresses, he thought my behaviour perfectly suitable. And so did I.

"Did they say who the guests are?" I asked her.

"Only that they were planning to come and visit Salt House, Lady Ilsaletta," she said.

I nodded, thinking. "In that case, Betsy, you'd best take to your bed. I think you may very well be sick, and Mistress Andza can hardly fault you for wanting to keep the sickness from the household with guests almost upon our doorstep."

She agreed and left and I turned to this very window, wondering how long I had until I would have to receive these visitors – a task I did poorly. I am not very social – when there was a commotion below.

It happened so fast that I hardly had time to think. A man leapt from the shadows and lunged for the captain of our house guard – right there below the window. The captain shouted for help and his men came running and I thought that would settle it – but half of them turned on him and the others.

"I won't look down at them," I whisper to Vargaard, "but if you stretch yourself, I'm sure you'll see what remains of them on the ground beneath the window."

I go back to telling the story in my mind.

Captain Arnault was still fighting for his life when the screaming started inside the house. I locked the door to the study. It was too late to run. And I couldn't escape through a window with enemies in the courtyard below. I shuttered the windows, grabbed the food and water and my father's hidden box – the one with the sword inside – and a few items from in his desk and that's where I've been ever since.

I've tried to leave this room twice – and twice I've had to hide again. There are still some who are not dead of either the sickness or the violence it causes – but all those who grow ill either fall dead or fall to wickedness. At least, as far as I can tell.

That's why we must leave – as quickly as possible. We don't dare stay.

There's a long silence and I'm beginning to worry that he isn't listening when he finally shifts inside my mind.

Gather anything you think you might need from this room. Start with the sword, then check the bodies for things you can use – knives, flint, coins – anything. We cannot stay in this room. The bodies attract attention. Bring that book of maps you had. Is there anything else you need from this room?

My father keeps an important book. It was what I was sneaking a look at when the sickness came. I left it on the desk.

Then bring that, too.

Won't he need it when he returns?

There will be nothing left of this place. If you think he may want it back, then keep it with you.

With shaking hands, I search Herrault's body, tears flowing as I slip off his blood-stained belt and belt pouch. There is flint in the pouch, and he has a small but sturdy camp knife.

It's well to feel – that keeps you human – but you don't have time to feel right now. Wrap up all those emotions into a knot and set them aside in your mind. You can return to them later when there is time for them.

I try to do what he says, and the tears lessen enough that I can see as I work. Havestock has a scabbard on his belt. That could be useful for the sword, but I hesitate over his body, fighting the urge to gag.

Leave it. There will be other scabbards. Bind the books with the belt so your sword hand is free. We may need to fight our way free of this place.

I can't fight. Herrault was a mistake and Havestock …

Calm down. Deep breaths.

I steady my breathing as I cinch the belt around the map book, but my father's secret book isn't here. I search the room, but it's not in the chaos around me. I will have to leave without it.

I can protect you, but only if you follow my instructions. You must be brave and firm because I can only reach as far as my shadow can stretch around you – which means that if you stumble backwards, it will pull me back, too. If you freeze in fright, I can't lunge forward. We must work together.

I can do that. I can work with him. I just need a minute. I breathe through my mouth, long, full breaths, eyes closed. All the horror and fear of the last few days is roaring over me, but I have to find enough courage in myself to leave this room. The urge to stay and hide is powerful. It claws down into my belly like a small animal seeking escape. It conjures images in my mind of safety. But there is no safety here.

Your safety is in my hands. You can entrust it to me.

But why is he doing this for me? How do you trust someone whose motives you don't understand?

I remember – darkness and then light. I was in that box. I was there so long that I've forgotten much but I remember my name. Vargaard of the Spineheights. I am Nakuraki and I am reborn today as your guardian and the warrior of your shadow. And I remember my vow to you. Do not fear, mortal girl. I will spill my life down to the last breath to keep you safe. Know it. It is truth come to life.

I swallow down apprehension because there is no other choice for me except to cower here and die. Is that all I am? A mouse waiting to be stomped on? A bug waiting to be smeared across the wall? I must be more.

I grip the hilt of the sword and raise my chin defiantly.

I am Ilsaletta Redtide. My father is Admiral Redtide of the Kingdom of Cragspear. I will not die as a mouse in the darkness.

Keep the tip of the sword high. Follow my instructions.

My sword is sharp. My grip is firm. I dare not let it be otherwise.

I fumble with the broken door and open it, wincing as the hinges squeak.

I am still shattered inside, but shattered glass can slice.

I step into Salt House.

Nakuraki

She blazes like a lost star. Bright and full. It draws from me a burning hope – a sense of opening and blossoming that makes my pulse speed. I feel as though I am remembering something lost, as though I've finally found something I have been searching for all along.

Confusion crashes in and then it, too, is washed away by certainty.

I want nothing more than to cling close to her – unless it's to keep her safe, to spill whatever a shadow has for blood in her service, in her honor, for her glory.

I strain to remember my other lives. They glint to me like fragments of windows shattered. I feel a dance of emotions – anger, fear, jealousy and with them come flashes of faces and places and my death by a thousand different hands but none of them resonate with this new tie that binds me to the bright shining mortal.

In my tattered memories, there are none that fit this shape.

This is new.

And I am made new by it.

Chapter Four

When it is this late in the afternoon, the servants begin to light the candles. They had been lit the night of my birthday and they are burned down to nubs, dripping wax trailing from their sconces.

I don't need the light of the candles but seeing them like this is chilling. Every morning of my life someone has cut away the nubs and replaced the candles. Seeing them like this is like watching someone dig up a grave.

Steady now. We need to find supplies and horses. Do you have a room in this house?

His voice in my mind almost caresses it every time he speaks leaving little chills of a completely different variety. There's something about the buzz of its resonance that goes through my mind and almost compels me to physically respond to his every suggestion. I'm already moving before I think.

My room is at the other end of the hall. It's a short journey but it feels like crossing the entire village. Every door down the hall is set open and the polished wood of the hall floor is marred by footprints. People with mud on their feet have walked through the house. And some of the mud is dark and crusted in a way that mud around here never is.

I hate the silence. It's worse than shouting with the potential it carries. I try to hold my breath. I need to listen for any sounds that might tell me there are others alive in these rooms. But my heart hammers so loudly in my chest that I hear nothing but its thunder.

I have fought in a thousand battles. Always, it is like this. You must find the way of the feather.

And what was that?

Deep breaths. Do not think of the next task or the task after that. Think only of what you do now. As the feather drifts upon the air, so you drift. Right now, in this moment, there is no threat here, there is only a long hallway to walk down. Take a step. Breathe.

I can take a step.

I take one.

Ease your feet quietly. Settle the weight on the ball of the foot – light as a feather. Soundless.

I concentrate on being soundless. Someone has broken the Gregoire vase that sits on the carved red fir table the Admiral brought back from the Crusted Shores. The tapestry depicting the gift of Spring is spattered all over with blood.

But I am a feather. I drift on the wind.

Good.

I summon my courage and pass the first door. I don't want to go into that room – a spare room for guests – but I want to know if anyone is in it. I try to peer within the door while stepping light as a feather.

Eyes ahead, novice warrior. I will look for you. He pauses. *There is a girl dead on the floor. She is about your size and perhaps a few years older. Dark hair like yours, just as long but gathered in a braid. White apron.*

Betsy.

She bears no marks of violence.

She had been ill. Had she left the study only to make it this far?

She has been dead for days. This is not for you to see. Walk on.

I might not see the body, but I can smell death. It fills my nose and makes me gag all the way down the hall. And I do not look in the rooms. I let Vargaard look for me. If I look – I will abandon the way of the feather and I will panic and run.

Be the feather. Do not run. If you run, you will be heard. There is only this moment. You are at the end of the hallway. Nothing is threatening you in this moment.

Had he spent every battle like this?

Yes.

And he'd survived them.

In a manner of speaking.

That does not comfort me.

The door to my room is closed. I place a hand on the door, take a deep breath, and push it open. I almost gasp when the room is empty. Relief is a powerful sensation. It clears the mind as quickly as the scent of snow.

I hurry within the room. I will need a travel cloak, a change of clothing, a satchel to carry it in, and a blanket for sleeping out of doors.

Calm down. You are going too fast. We are not out of danger yet.

But here in my own room, I can almost pretend it was all a bad dream. That when I go back out again cook will be busy over the evening meal and Betsy will be lighting the hall candles.

I snatch up a leather satchel from inside my wardrobe and fill it with a change of clothes, extra underthings, a few smaller personal items, and the book of maps from my father's study. I roll up a wool blanket, tie it with a belt, and then stuff it in the top of the satchel. I attach the knife I took on one of my wider belts, dump the contents of the belt pouch into my own pouch and add what coin and jewelry I have – very little. It will have to be enough to feed me along the road. I strap the sword sheath to my belt and buckle it but when I move to sheathe the sword, the Nakuraki hisses.

Keep it out. Even untrained, you are safter with it in your hands.

I swallow. All I need now is a cloak. I reach for my closet door.

When you open the door, step back immediately.

It seems an odd request, but I open the door and step back all in one motion.

Something tumbles from the closet and my hand clasps around my mouth holding the scream inside.

I can't. I can't breathe.

I want to scream, and scream, and scream until I die.

If I scream, I *will* die.

I let a breath shudder out of me instead.

It's Cook. Her eyes are wide open. She clutches a kitchen knife in her hand but she's dead and cold and … heaven send mercy, she doesn't look right.

We'll get a cloak from somewhere else. Your father's room, perhaps.

His voice in my mind caresses me, but it's not enough to erase what I just saw. I'm never going to be able to close my eyes again without seeing her face.

Heaven send mercy, her face.

She's not in there. It's only a shell. Shells wither and rot but she does not feel it. You need not feel it either.

But I do. I do.

Out into the hall. Move. Now.

I abandon any pretense of thinking for myself and do what I'm ordered. It's easier this way. Easier than thinking.

Your father's room. Which is it?

I stumble my way down the hall to the door. It's open and that somehow feels less safe than if it was shut. But there's no one inside and he has his large brass-buttoned naval coats and thick cloaks hung up on a coat tree. I shrug on the coat and sling a dark charcoal cloak over it. The cloak hood is lined with fur and it smells like him – tobacco and the lemon oil they use to polish the wood of his ships.

And now we leave. Remember the way of the feather and keep your sword tip up.

It's easier to pretend it isn't happening. That it isn't me walking down the broad staircase and flinching at every squeak – that it isn't me who is stepping over the bloated bodies of people I once knew. And it's even easier if I talk to him, so I do.

Vargaard?

Yes, mortal girl?

Where do you come from?

There is a pause as we reach the bottom of the stairs. I know he's looking in every direction before he steers me toward the great hall. We must pass through it to leave the house this way. The servants' entrance would be faster, but this house has many servants and most of them will be in there – one way or another.

The gaps in my memory are vast. And I am no longer that man. When I say I am reborn, I mean that literally. This is the first day of this life. But I do remember a kingdom called Rastara where I was Nakuraki to a queen. She danced the Blood Fire dance for a visiting noble. And I danced in her shadow.

I've never seen Rastara on my father's maps.

Perhaps Geer'd'an? I have a sliver of a memory of that place. A monk, I think, held my bond. He led an army to take over the steppe barons.

Monks leading armies? I thought monks retreated from the world to find peace.

Not these monks. The world retreated from them *if it wanted peace.*

Hmm. I have not heard of Geer'd'an either. But I would rather think of warrior monks and dancing queens right now than what I am seeing. I refuse to look directly at the many people piled against the walls in the Great Hall. But even in my peripheral I still see too much. Most have died of violence. Most are guards. If I look closely, I will surely recognize some.

I can hear my own whimper building but Vargaard cuts it off.

Perhaps something newer. I recall a scrap of memory about Emperor of Deiven Ras Chasten. He held my sword in his fist and bid me dance the lilt of blades at his command. He was known as the Monkey of the Seven Isles and I have other memories – glimpses of his children and grandchildren – all ugly in the same way.

A hiss catches in my throat. I'm so startled that it pulls me out of this moment entirely. I have read of Deiven Ras Chasten. That empire passed over five hundred years ago and ended in a long, drawn-out war of succession.

Vargaard seemed more than usually silent at that revelation. Was that the most recent memory he had?

I have been trapped in that box for a very long time. The mind howls to think of it. And yet it is not me, but only what came before.

I'm at the front doors of the grand entrance. The ancestral chandelier hangs above my head. The colored panes in the doors shine bright on my skin. I must open them and go out into the night – and yet I am terrified to do it. If so many horrors lay within, what will lay without?

We must find a horse. Who knows how far this disease has spread? We may need to move far and fast.

A horse. I can focus on that.

I push the door open. It catches on something. I push again and manage to move it enough to squeeze through. Vomit rises in my mouth as I look down and I turn to the side. I spill it all over the other door.

A guard died defending the door. Or at least – that's the story I will tell myself and I will *not* think of how much of him is missing.

A terrible battle was fought here. He pauses, sounding confused. *I … I think I have seen this once before.*

He has? Surprise jolts through me. He's seen this madness before? This is not something I have heard of. It's not something I can fathom at all. How does a disease turn one man against another? And what was that pink smoke?

That man was possessed. I remember that much, though the details are opaque. Something about a green gem and a fever that catches. Some of the population die immediately. Others turn into something unrecognizable and they slay those around them.

What do they turn into?

It's on the edge of my thoughts but I can't grasp it. Something terrible.

Nothing can be more terrible than how things already are.

I take hesitant steps across the courtyard, focusing on the way of the feather. I am in this moment. I am not thinking about what comes next. I need a horse.

But there are so many dead here that it is hard to stay in the moment. I must keep my mind busy.

Vargaard?

Yes?

Are you made of shadow?

Yes. Shadow and soul.

I have yet to see him. Here in the courtyard, my shadow is long. I turn and look. He rises from my shadow, a dark humanoid figure, slender but well-muscled, dressed in shadow clothing in a shape I do not recognize. His face, his eyes, his hair

– all of it dark, nearly transparent shadow.

He flickers as he changes rapidly from one form to another – all of them look like a man in his early twenties, his features refined and beautiful, eyes wide and haunted and mouth quirked slightly as if curiosity is his greatest attribute.

But as I watch his hair is long and short, shorter yet, shaved on one side and then pulled into a queue, braided, and then short again. And his face flickers, too – whole and then with a bandage over one eye like a pirate story, then without the eye and then whole all over again.

And his clothing jumps from one style to another to still another and at one point it leaves him entirely except for a small breechcloth and a pair of bracers, and my face flares hot at the sight of all of him at once.

I'm grateful when it settles again on a well-cut jacket of a foreign style with a high collar and though it is open and he wears no shirt underneath, at least he's wearing a broad cloth wrapped around his waist like a belt and black breeches. His shadow seems to like this shape the best. It stays for a full breath before flickering again.

And through it all, dark shadows flow through his shape like the swirls and eddies of the river as it caresses the rocks just under its surface.

I reach toward him, wondering if he is real to the touch, and he dances back.

You will not be able to touch me. Your hand will pass right through.

My throat bobs uncomfortably.

How does he fight for me if he cannot be touched?

Only in violence do I become corporeal enough to affect the world and only while the violence lasts.

Fear shudders through me.

You should be afraid. I am fearsome indeed.

And now he will lurk forever in my shadow.

I prefer the term "reside," but I suppose that I shall agree to "lurk" if you prefer.

The shadowy smile he gives me is crooked. I'm grateful for the distraction.

And how far can you stretch?

This far. He reaches out to the side, his body elongating slightly, a shadow weapon appearing in his hands, but his feet are locked to my shadow as he shifts into what I know is a sword form, even though I couldn't explain which discipline it is from. He moves again to a new sword form and then another. And then he twists around me. I turn to follow his movement and realize he can wrap right around me and almost touch his shadow on the other side – but we are very close, our trembling breaths one as he is spread thin against me.

He catches the edge of his bottom lip in his shadow teeth as if waiting for me to cry out in alarm.

And I feel nothing. He was right. He is not corporeal. He is shadow and thought. He is wisdom and loyalty. But he has no body. Were I to ask for the comfort of it, he could not embrace me – or rather, I could not feel it if he did.

It's tragic. I try to push the thought from my mind.

He bites his shadow lip harder and I swear it turns white

under the pressure.

Ignoring the truth helps nothing. I am Nakuraki.

And have you always been Nakuraki?

He pauses, his shadowy brow furrowed.

I remember cherry blossoms and laughter and a large dog. I remember kind hands helping me walk. Was I a shadow then? I do not know. What I was has passed. I am now today, born to a new life.

And I know only Salt House and the town of Saltfast below.

So do I.

And everything else I know is from books – other people's memories.

Again, we are alike.

If only I knew something practical.

Do you know how to ride a horse?

I do know that. I ride for pleasure most days. I have a beautiful dapple all my own by the name of Moonlight. We take the cave paths down from Salt House to the beach and we ride and ride with the wind in our hair and faces. Her hooves smack the sand, and her snorts fill my heart.

I can almost smell the surf as I remember it. We'll leave as soon as I find Moonlight. Vargaard won't even need his own horse. He will ride with me.

I will ride with you from now on, he says, and I swear there's a smirk in his tone. *You're fortunate. You will save coin on food and horseflesh since I am the only retainer who requires neither.* He pauses and grows sober. *Is this passage through the stables to the beaches the only way up to this fortress of a house?*

I have never considered the house a fortress, though it is built into the stone. I've always thought of it as a nest perched above the sea. But I see what he means. It would be hard to attack this place by any normal means. The disease, however, is not deterred by our defenses. It is the only kind of siege we were not prepared to withstand.

There were two entrances – one through the winding cavern carved from the beach to the stables. It was partially filled with water when the tides were high, and my father installed a steel grill gate as further defense – but it is never locked. The other entrance was a winding road that exited into town. There is no way off the road since either side of it is so steep that calling it a cliff is charitable.

Worrisome.

Why is that? I bite my lip as we reach the stable. I don't like how quiet it is. I'm used to the sound of stable hands working, of guards and servants coming and going. This is where the guards train, their muscled bodies hard from practice and their voices loud and excitable. I won't admit how often I've watched them secretly from behind the pages of a book.

I doubt it was much of a secret.

My cheeks are already hot as he says that.

And the reason it's worrisome is because everyone will know that there are only two exits in and out of this place. That's great if you are defending it – but a problem if you are trying to sneak out unnoticed. Especially with a horse.

Would anyone be alive to watch for us?

I always assume someone is watching everything and that they are watching with the intent to kill or harm my Vali.

How pessimistic.

I'd say it kept them alive, but I would not be your guardian if I were still theirs. I have a thousand failures to learn from. They will slowly trickle back to me and I will feel every one of them again as if it is happening for the first time. And with every reminder, I will learn a lesson on how to keep you from their fates.

Did he remember a plan like ours? A situation like this one? I feel so jittery, I'm surprised I can breathe steadily. Everything inside me wants to work its way out.

His words are slightly rasping and pained when he says. *The siege of A'ha'raihm. It was like this. There were only two ways into the fortress. They coated the main gates with pitch and lit them on fire. For days we battled the flames, but eventually, we admitted our failure. We were forced to take the other entrance. They were waiting for us there. They cut down my Vali. Her blood sank into the sand.*

I shudder at his words and I shudder at what I'm seeing here in the entrance to the stables.

Flies.

More flies than I've ever seen before. And they cling to their own dark spot on the sand. And now I'm realizing why it feels too quiet. There are no snorts or whickers from within. There are no sounds of munching hay or lapping water.

I don't want to look.

Sometimes the terror we fear is worse than the terror that is.

I open the door to the stables and I look.

But he is wrong. The terror I feared was not half what is there. And I cannot go inside. Even if I could, there would be no way I could pull a stack of a dozen dead horses from in front of the entrance to the caverns. I would need another horse to do that.

I don't even realize I'm crying until my vision starts to blur and my eyes sting.

Nakuraki

Her tears are diamonds dripping, stalactites forming of my failure to guard her from this.

I swallow as I realize she is no new goddess but a fragile mortal – only a breath away from death. Still, she shines bright as a new dawn.

Precious.

And breakable.

And with terrible realization I see that if she breaks, I will break, too, and not just to retreat back into the sword. I will end with her end. I will die with her death. I must hold her close and take every blow aimed for her. I must shield her and shelter her and succor her.

And I will. The vows I made are unbreakable. Even given to a mortal and not a goddess.

I do not regret them.

After the passing of two more dawns, I will be hers.

Chapter Five

We are halfway down the road to Saltfast before I manage to stop sobbing. My sobs have been silent, but they have left me dull and listless. I wonder if I should have died up there, too.

Absolutely not. Do not be a coward.

Coward? I am not that. I am just exhausted and worn down from fear and horror and I cannot stand one more moment of it.

We all grow tired from time to time. The brave dig deep and find a reason to go on. Cowards sit down and sleep and never again rise.

His words sting. Anyone else who just hid for days and then saw everyone they knew in piles on the ground would be just as upset as I am right now. And they would be afraid.

I know the town will be just as bad. And I will have to pass through at least some of it to get out. We will have to go to the Saltfast stables to see if any horses remain alive.

And then what do you want, my Vali? Your dreams are my future.

My lower lip trembles. I just want to go home. But there is no home anymore. I want my father. What if he comes back here and finds this before I find him? Will he sift through the dead looking for me?

We shall find him.

For now, I just want to go somewhere that isn't here.

Deep breaths. Embrace the way of the feather. We need only go to these stables and then we will flee. Perhaps, we can also find food and water for your journey.

I should have collected those at the house. But just thinking of going to the Salt House kitchens makes my stomach lurch. Cook and Herrault wouldn't have fled the kitchens if there hadn't been something to flee.

I fight down nausea and force myself to keep going. Stay in the moment. One step at a time. One breath at a time.

I keep the tip of my blade up in the air. Why has such a fine sword been locked in a box all this time? Why do they think it is evil? Other than its black blade – rippled like Damascus steel, but black on black – it looks like a normal sword. The blade is single-edged and slightly curved, the handle large enough for two hands and swathed in black silk, but it doesn't glow ominously, or sing when it is drawn from a scabbard, or suck all light into its depths.

It is a valuable blade by its own right. I doubt they would have locked it up except that it was inhabited by me.

So, it really is Vargaard they want locked away.

I will never stop being amazed at humans. The things you think are astonishing. I have no wish to hurt my wielder and no wish to hurt anyone she does not wish to destroy.

Does he sound evil?

Evil or good, it is too late to be rid of me. The vows have been said. I have my home in your shadow.

But he can just as easily move to someone else's. What if someone steals the blade?

Best to avoid that.

I'm certain that if I leave it here on the side of the road, I will lose his protection.

It's not wise to discard your best weapon when surrounded by enemies.

Why attach his future to a blade at all?

Think, mortal girl. Why would you do it?

I lick my lips and I think. He would be less versatile and flexible bound to the shadow of a blade than bound to a less moveable object. Was it so that they could pass him from one person to another?

That's part of it.

So that he could protect whoever was most vulnerable?

A charitable interpretation.

So that one of them wasn't stuck with him living in their shadow forever? Hovering there while they ate and drank. Sleeping beside them at night and hearing every conversation.

There it is.

I shiver even though I am not cold. I have just described what I have agreed to when he made vows to me and I gave him my blood.

I had no choice.

No. I will not accept that from you. You had a choice. You had the freedom to pick. You picked me because I am the best choice.

I picked him so I could live.

Living is often the best choice.

I'm still mulling on the idea that most of the big choices we make in life are made without enough thought and wondering if my father is going to be furious with me and what it means that we have a deeper link than simply the sword, when I take the first step into the village. Even if I didn't know all was not well, I'd know now.

The village is never silent. It is loud and obnoxious even at night. People drink and sing ribald songs. Roosters crow – it's a myth that they reserve that for the dawn – babies scream, and people slam doors and fight and laugh. In the day it is worse with the fishermen coming and going on the docks and the hawkers shouting wares while the blacksmith hammers.

Not today. Today I hear a hinge squeaking as the wind saws the door back and forth. Someone's laundry is half hung on the line and half strewn across the road and that which is strewn is trampled in dark, crusted footprints.

The silence eats into my bones.

I want to run. I want to loop around the mill to my right and run as hard as I can out of the village and into the hills. But if I don't get food and water and a good horse, how far will I go? How far did the villagers go? How many are out there in the woods right now? Changing. Lurking.

My heart is a lump of ice and I want it to stay like that. Don't melt. Don't smash. Don't beat at all. It's not worth it.

Dark descends so suddenly that I clutch at my throat in surprise.

Easy. It is only dusk. I am not gone. I will walk with you. He pauses as I step further into the street. *I have a scrap of memory of a time when our city was overrun by the Hoons – barbarians from the east. Falcet – my Vali – was dancing the quaranda with a lady of the Galvea Valley when the news broke into the ballroom. They had breached the walls. They were pouring over the city, pillaging and burning as they went. Falcet was afraid. I felt his fear as I feel yours now. But he did not hesitate. He took the lady's hand, drew his sword, and fought his way through the streets to the Eastern Wall to take her to safety. His courage was the courage of lions. He did not fall until the last of the women with them were safe and fleeing the city with the castle guard. He and five others stayed to cover their retreat. I fought with the fury of seven winds and Falcet fought with the fury of one desperate mortal soul, until – at last – we were overrun by hundreds. It was a stand of the ages.*

And he'd ended up dead. Just like the crumpled form I am stepping over.

I try not to look. I choke on a sob.

The streets of Saltfast are just like Salt House. People lay where they fell. And they fell everywhere. The fruit merchant's cart is whirling with fruit flies, the fruit sits in stacks where it was put out for sale. It is spoiled by the hot sun. The butcher's cart stinks, the meat long spoiled, but still hung for purchase. I swallow at the sight and force my feet to move. I must not linger. I must not dwell. I must concentrate. I have a single goal.

Yes, he died – but a life like that! A death like that! He was a true hero. I'm glad to remember him.

Did he want to be a hero like that, or was he just a man in the wrong place at the wrong time who refused to quit?

A light flares in the diamond-paned windows of the inn. I freeze in the street.

Someone is alive.

Vargaard is talking to me but I'm not hearing him. My heartbeat is too loud. The darkness clouding my vision is too overwhelming. I can't breathe. I can't breathe.

Pain flares across my face and I flinch. They're here. They're attacking me already. I lunge with my sword but there's nothing in front of me. Someone is crying. It's me. I sound like a wet rag ripping.

Another burst of pain as if I've been slapped and I stop. My chest is heaving. I need to catch a breath. Sweet, sweet air fills my lungs. I cling to the sensation and finally, I can hear his voice.

… apologies and you can punish me for it later, but you must get yourself under control. Panic is the warrior's most severe enemy.

I am no warrior.

You were not before, but now by fate or by design, you have become one.

My molars rattle with my shaking but he doesn't let up.

Get back in the shadows. Avoid that light. They must not know you are here. I remember Shagrin.

What is Shagrin?

Here, tuck in here. That's right. Can you see the entrance to the stable?

I nod. There is no light there. I can sneak up to it, but I will have to pass the inn to get there unless I want to circle around, going further out of my way. And who knows what horrors may lie on other streets. Or who else might yet live.

But why is anyone still alive. Should they not all be dead by now – either of the disease or of the violence?

You are not dead.

I hadn't caught it, though. I hadn't been close enough to Betsy and then I'd been in the closet.

You aren't in the closet anymore. But if you are ill, we will face that when it comes. Slip to the alley and stay out of the light. You can duck low and pass along the rear side of the inn. That will be where the door to the kitchens is set – the best potential place to find unspoiled food and water.

No. That will put me close to whoever is there.

It's also the most direct route to those stables.

I let a sigh puff through my lips.

Let your feet take you forward and concentrate on my story. It is coming back to me in little scraps, but it will help to keep your mind off what you do. The story of Shagrin starts with the king's chancellor.

Don't they all?

I worry my lip between my teeth and settle on the balls of my feet to creep below the windows of the inn. I'm not muscular or tough – not a warrior in any way. I am wisp thin and my brown skin is smooth and soft. I do not cut my hair or braid it back tightly as I've seen female guards and sailors do. It swirls around me like black silk. I am soft and graceful and utterly feminine – made for reading old dusty books and taking careful notes, not for violence and physical labor.

We do what we must, even if it goes against what we were made for. And so did the people of Shagrin, when they realized they had been betrayed. Counselor Wu'shande Avien Duchalis was known through all of Shagrin as an ambitious man. It was he who brought the gaming wheels to Shagrin and the bright green orrin bulbs with the smoke they made that dulled the mind. The populace adored him, waiting in tender anticipation for the next great thing he would reveal.

The kitchen door is open, and hams hang in nets along the wall with baskets of onions and carrots, flatbread, and bowls of yogurt.

Take the meat and flatbread. Leave the vegetables and yogurt. It's too bulky. Is that a pot of honey? Take that, too.

I slip into the inn, biting my lip hard as I try to be soundless. I am not heavy, but I have no practice in sneaking anything except for books out of my father's library.

Thievery is always costly.

I freeze, hand over the flatbread.

I don't mean you. I'm still telling the story. If you don't steal this food from the dead, they will feast on your withered corpse.

Counsellor Wu'shande, however, had no need to break into the tombs of the Isahn people as he did – or to steal from their gods. But the gods of the Ishan had been placed beneath the ground in caverns larger than cities. And their tombs were filled with rich treasures – golden images, painted masks, and more gems that any one person ever needs. They sacked the tombs, slew every Isahn they found, and set their cities to the flame. But Counsellor Wu'shande took one prize for himself – an emerald the size of your fist that glowed with a strange black light.

There's an empty waterskin in the corner and I snatch it, too.

But I hear a board creak and I freeze.

Vargaard goes silent.

"… food," a voice says as it approaches. It is not a voice I know. It is a rich voice used to giving orders. "And something to drink for Princess Jendaya. She remains upstairs in her room behind that locked door and surely even she will need water. Then check on Gayreth and his men in the stables. Those horses are our lives. If a single one falls, it will slow our flight."

My breath is caught in my throat. I don't dare take another.

"You don't think it's slowed already?" another voice asks, insolent and masculine.

"I think it was good that we tried this here first. We will know what to expect when we reach Swordheart. Who would have thought it would be so difficult to hold back the husks? Next time, we must be more ready. We lost far too many in the initial surge."

Next time? It seems there are plotters here, as well.

But I am not thinking of plotters or husks. I am thinking of a violet pressed between the pages of a book and a black velvet dress and a yellow canary. I am thinking of being eight years old with a living mother and going for a trip to the Summer Palace along the sea and eating honey cakes in my special dress and then playing with a little girl the exact same size as me – a little girl with huge brown eyes and a wicked smile who dared me to open the door of the canary cage.

I haven't seen that girl in ten years, but I'll never forget Princess Jendaya. No one who meets her ever does.

And she's here. Up in a room. It sounds like she is their prisoner.

You can't afford to be distracted. Not if you're going to escape. I hear footsteps. When I say "go" you will dash out the door and then step to the side and press your back to the wall.

Her dress had been blue. She'd laughed when the canary flew back.

"It likes the cage," she'd said.

Go!

I'm dashing out the door. I'm pressing my back to the wall. But I'm thinking of that laughing girl. What is she doing in Saltfast? Who are these men who keep her locked in a room?

In the end, Wu'shande called them husks, too.

My shadow sounds like he's brooding about something, which suits my mood perfectly. Now is not the time to run. Now is the time to stop and consider.

You have food and water. All we need is a horse. There will always be princesses and they will always be locked up or married against their will or sold for land and riches and none of that need trouble you.

I thought he said that I was a warrior now.

Not like this.

I thought he said I needed to dig in deep and find courage.

Not this kind. He sounds worried.

He should be worried. Because I see another light on the second story of the inn. And a plan is already beginning to blossom in my mind.

Nakuraki

My memories return in slivers – glimpses into a life I once had. But they are the memories of someone else. I am none of those people now. I don't want to be.

But I let the memories come. I sift them and sort them and take what I can in the constant stream of sensations. They blend together and tangle up like strands of rope left in the same basket. I cannot tell where one begins and another ends.

I am not afraid. These memories do not anchor me. Who I once was – all those thousands of other iterations of Vargaard – that is not who I am. I am who she needs me to be.

I am a bather in the heat of her sun, a prostrate worshipper in the temple of her light.

I remember emotions before and as they ripple through me now, I can name them – anger is that hot flash and fear that stab of cold. Jealousy is the one that clouds my thoughts and chokes in my throat. Relief is like a calm sea and a breath of fresh air.

And among them is one I do not know, one that makes my heart squeeze and my breath catch and my hands tremble. I have not yet learned the nature of it. There is no feeling like it in the shards of memory I sift through.

I feel it every time I look at her.

CHAPTER SIX

Six guards surround the stable. Vargaard steers me around it, counting them. There's something wrong with the one we're watching right now from a nearby alley. He leans down to check his boot and he moves strangely – like he doesn't quite fit in his skin.

He's a husk now – a corricle. That's what I remembered about Shagrin. People like him, shambling around. He's not a man anymore, he just holds a space in this world for someone from the next world to rush in and fill the void.

A ghost? I squint my eyes. A fly walks over the guard's forehead and he ignores it. He doesn't care. Maybe he's past caring.

Not a ghost – the avatar of someone from the beyond. Ghosts are sad things clinging to this life. These are more than that. They are the strongest of the strong. They have fought off their brothers to rend the walls of their world and return to ours.

His throaty voice is low in my mind and I find myself hanging on it, compelled to listen to every word and convinced to believe him.

Do you believe in reincarnation, Vargaard?

His mind shivers at my thought and I wish I could see him, but the light here is so low that he blends into the shadow so I only see a flicker of movement on the edges of my vision.

Only for myself. Everyone else I have watched die has crossed over to the other side. And sometimes crossed back – but they are the same mind moving back and forth. Me? I am not. I am new every time.

I pause. That sounds like torture. To lose yourself and have to start over again and again. To never progress. To forget who you were.

Truly, I am cursed.

There's a ripple in his husky voice and I'm sorry that I mentioned it.

Face hot with shame, I turn back to what I should be doing.

The fly on the guard's forehead has been joined by two more. Behind the guard, a horse whickers and something like longing stirs inside me. That horse means freedom. It means possibility. My hands itch at the thought of taking up his reins.

We'll take one at the right moment and then we'll be gone, Vargaard assures me, but I am not convinced.

I can't just run like a coward.

Be reasonable, you are a new warrior and I am relearning my way. We should not attack a group of armed warriors of unknown numbers and allegiance. You are too precious to waste like a wave upon the shore.

I'm touched. But I can't leave Jendaya to these people.

Why not? What is she to you?

She is nothing to me except a girl I knew for a day. But he

couldn't leave me to die locked in a closet and I can't leave her to the same fate. I feel him shift and something about it seems guilty.

Had you not held the sword and opened the box, I would not have taken you as my Vali. Surely, you are light to me, as the guiding star of the north to my soul, but I risked nothing in that choice and you will risk everything in this one.

He chose me, though, and he has been kind ever since. Now, Jendaya needs someone to be kind to her. Has Vargaard fought these husks before? Did he stand up to the Counsellor's men when he made husks like this before?

I feel him shift again and this time the sense that he is ashamed comes through our connection so powerfully that I feel my own face blushing.

Just because a Nakuraki is a shadow does not mean it is free of pain.

So, he did fight them, and he lost, and the pain of it is too great to bear.

That is not what I am claiming. I did not stand against the infected. I did not fight.

Then why do his words make me think that he holds the weight of all of history on his shadowed shoulders?

I was Nakuraki to Wu'shande. I watched as he breathed on the gem and inhaled the scent of it. I watched as the sickness took him — and as he gave it to everyone else. It spread like fire. It could not be contained.

My breath hitches in my throat. I hear another horse whinny. I don't want to know this about Vargaard.

I do not always choose the right side, Vali.

And he is not choosing it now. The princess needs our help.

Let me at least choose right with you. Let me keep you safe.

I clench my fist so hard that my fingernails sink into the flesh and I blink back tears. I am afraid to die. I am afraid of pain. I don't want to know what it's like to feel my life slipping away.

And yet.

What is survival if it means doing things you can't live with? I can barely live with Herrault's death at my hands. When I close my eyes, I see him lying on the floor.

If I run right now, I will see Jendaya in my mind forever and I will imagine all the things they did to her before she died. And I will know they are all my fault.

No. Don't do that. What others have done is not your shame to bear.

Isn't he doing the same thing? He says he is new and born fresh and yet he feels guilt for what those other Vargaard's did.

That seems to halt his objections. I leave him to muse over them and I glance back up at the inn.

My belly flips and nausea creeps up. I'm shaking all over, sweat breaking out across my forehead and my back. I have known terror these past few days. It returns to me like an old friend. It melts under my skin like dripping snow. I let it rise, but I do not let it conquer.

I ease myself back into the shadows. I will need to get her before I get a horse. If I take the horses first, someone will know.

Horses? It's harder to steal two than just one. I can't guarantee success.

I ignore him and set my satchel carefully in the alley next to the wall. It will slow me down for this next part. I sheathe my sword.

No, this is a terrible idea, mortal girl. This will get you killed. I can only do so much to help you. Bring the sword back out.

To my relief, he did not disappear when I sheathed it. I thought he might.

But I am determined. I am a good climber. When the rest of the house is at work, I have time on my hands. I often run along the beaches and scale the sea cliffs so I may watch the waves break out from the shore and feel the wind on my hair. I can scale the side of the inn. There are ledges and large exposed timbers.

Someone will hear you. Or see you. Especially if you are using window ledges to climb.

I dart across the street and back to the side of the inn. She has made it easy for me with her lit candle. I know which room is hers.

You are mad! Even if you get up there, how will you get her down?

We will find a way once we are there.

No, no, no. This isn't happening. You must not do it!

What did he care? He would not die, even if I did. He could go back to the sword.

I have suffered long years in the shadow of the sword. Your mind, in comparison, is like sweet nectar and I have not drunk my fill. I beg you with all my soul, do not risk yourself to this madness.

I pause. So. Now he tells the truth. He has not been helping me out of altruism. Or pity. He is a creature who has served evil lords and masters and he is only helping me because of what he gains from it – access to my mind and thoughts.

Please.

It's hard to push back the velvet plea, but I ignore him. His judgment – flawed and selfish – will not guide me.

If you will not heed pleas, then heed a threat, his voice turns cold, *climb and I will not help you. Jump into the jaws of death and I will stand by and do nothing.*

I hate this choice. I do not want to make it. I am many things – soft and bookish, pampered and comfortable – but not selfish, or at least not so selfish that I would give another's life for my own.

I look up at the window and pause, listening. When I hear no one near, I set my foot on the ledge, grip the frame and push myself up. It will be a scramble, but I can do it.

My shadow is silent. He has made good on his threat and he is gone. With him, goes my sense of security and boldness. I bite my lip against rising anxiety and force myself to climb. It's the right decision. It's the only decision.

The exposed beams give me just enough purchase that even my skirts do not slow me. I may not be muscular, but I am light and flexible, and I use this to my advantage.

My arms are burning as I reach the end of a beam sticking through the plaster of the wall. It is level with the princess's window, but it will be a stretch to reach that far. I reach, leaning out as far as I can without letting go of the beam. My fingertips slip along the edge, but I can't quite catch it. I can lean further, but I'm not sure that I can get back to the beam if I do.

I take a deep breath. I've come this far. I must not turn back now.

I bite my lip and lunge for the window ledge. I catch it, but my legs slip from the beam and I fall, swinging as all my weight is transferred to my fingertips. My body crashes against the wall and I suck in a breath as my fingers slip against the ledge. I bite down hard on my lip and taste blood.

I feel a flutter of panic in the back of my mind that is not my own. But Vargaard can't help me. This is not an enemy he can defeat. It's just gravity.

Above me, the window squeaks open. I can't see who opened it. And no one speaks. If I pull myself up, there could just as easily be an enemy in that window as a princess. Or, I could drop.

It's a long drop.

Seizing every scrap of boldness that I have, I scrabble against the plaster wall with my feet and pull with all my might.

I clamber up the window ledge and pull myself over and through the window into the room, my momentum carrying me to the floor. I roll, come to my feet in a tangle of skirts, and look up into a pair of very wide brown eyes.

They're exactly as I remembered them.

CHAPTER SEVEN

Princess Jendaya looks exactly as I expected from her fluttering azure veils to her golden ringlets. But she is much stronger than I would expect in a girl her size – stronger than me – and she pulls me up and into the room easily as if she greets visitors this way all the time.

"Princess," I gasp as I find my feet, sketching a hasty courtesy in my ridiculous man-sized cloak and coat. I hadn't thought to be embarrassed for my appearance until now. "I'm so glad you're alive."

"Are you?" she asks, her full lip trembling prettily. "I thought you were dead, Ilsaletta. We went to your house first and everyone there …" She shudders. "There were people piled up like drifts of leaves."

I don't want to think about people in drifts. I want to get out of here with her while she is still alive.

"We have to run," I whisper. She's standing so near that I haven't seen her room yet, just her wide eyes and innocent expression. I think she'll have to come out the window with me, but until I look around, I won't know for sure.

"But aren't you infected?" she asks, tilting her head to the side.

Her golden curls bounce. "Everyone seems to be infected."

"You aren't," I gasp. "We have to hurry before they know someone is here for you. We can sneak out the window and I have some supplies ready."

"The very good and the very bad don't die immediately. They make up roughly twenty percent of the population, all told," she says sweetly. Has her mind been addled by terror? "But most people are in the middle – not very good or very bad. Just people. Easily led, easily swayed … easily dead."

My stomach does a flip like it thinks it's an eel and my eyes narrow. Has she lost her mind? Or …

She steps backward and now I see her room. I feel like my stomach has dropped into my knees. Blood drains from my face, leaving me lightheaded so suddenly that I reach out for support.

Her room is not the room of a terrified captive. There are no ropes for binding her or a rumpled bed or water left on the floor or any of the things I was imagining.

What I notice first is the *real* captive. He's tied to rings on the wall that look just like the rings used in a stable to tie horses – and the wood around them is slightly chipped, the chipped areas lighter and brighter than the rest. Someone installed them very recently.

A wad of cloth has been stuffed in his mouth and his eyes are wide with terror. He twitches and I realize he can't move in his spread-eagle position against the wall. His black hair is in disarray, his face is shadowed in growth. He smells of fear sweat.

My mouth is suddenly dry.

"It turns out that the duke is good." Princess Jendaya's laugh freezes my heart. "Who would have thought? With his reputation as a notorious rake and layabout, I'd thought he'd be evil – or at the very least unremarkable."

I swallow and inch backward.

"Oh – I wouldn't do that," she says and lunges toward me. Something bright and silvery slashes through the air. "Falchion! Culverin! To me!"

My heart is in my throat. I stumble, tripping on something under my feet, and sprawl backward at the same moment that my shadow comes to life. My fall has saved me from the slash of the knife. Now, Vargaard rushes out from me, feet planted on the ground where the inky crescent of my real shadow lies. He rolls upward like a wave rushing to fill a hole dug in the sand, billows up upon it like gathering thunderheads, and then coalesces into something solid. It happens so fast that if I didn't know what Vargaard was, I wouldn't know what I'd seen. He is corporeal for but a breath – a perfect warrior in a defensive pose, his hard eyes focused, hands held out like they are weapons, too. His close-cropped hair swirls and he spins quickly, pinning the knife between flat palms and wrenching it away. He's beautiful like a porpoise arching up and leaping through the waves, like a heron stepping lightly through the reeds in the summer. I gasp at his grace and power and then he's gone again.

He's glorious and otherworldly and not even a little bit human.

Be reasonable. Don't try to rescue her. It's not worth your life.

Well, I'm certainly not trying to rescue her *now*.

I stumble backward one more time. The window is my only chance, or I'll be chained to the wall, too. I knock over a low table and fall, my hands clutching at anything nearby. They settle on a book and I hold it up in front of me like a shield as the men

Jendaya called come crashing into the room, weapons held high.

Of course, I will die trying to defend myself with a book. It's so predictable that I want to laugh. Or maybe cry. Or maybe just give up.

But I keep it held up before me like a talisman.

"Help our guest into a chair," the princess says brightly.

I glance to the window as they rush toward me – but even if I get to it in time – what will I do? It would take a minute to find my balance and leap for the beam – and then they'd have me. Or, I could jump out the window, but I'm high enough up that I'd break my legs. It will be harder to outrun them on a broken leg.

Would you like to leave now? I can help with that.

They seize my arms before I can answer and I am thrust unceremoniously into a comfortable padded chair.

Just to be clear, I am trying to respect your wishes, but I'm finding this very hard. It would be better if you chose to leave this place.

What did he think I was trying to do?

But you remain …

Because they grabbed my arms.

He leaps to life, his delicate features almost perfectly clear in his shadowy form, just as Princess Jendaya takes the chair opposite mine and begins to pour tea. He's right beside her chair. He reaches for her and –

No!

I barely get the thought out. He freezes, fingers still stretching toward her throat, a look of pure innocence on his face.

She's holding you captive now.

I want to sigh.

She is pouring tea, not sharpening her knives or tying a noose. I can probably refrain from murdering her until after she's said her piece.

The hard angles of his face look grim, but he pulls his hands back and fades back into nothing but shadow. I'm shocked that no one has noticed him. Stunned that the guards are so relaxed on either side of me.

He disappears.

Vargaard? I ask.

He does not reply. He must be angry with me. My stomach does a flip at the thought. I should have let him choke Princess Jendaya while he was still here to do it.

Jendaya sets the teapot back on the tray and smiles at me. It's exactly what I would have expected of a reunion with her – minus the guards holding my arms on either side of the chair and the man trying to yell through his gag chained to the wall.

"Set the book down, please Ilsaletta," Princess Jendaya says calmly.

I move to obey and freeze. In my hand, is my father's record book. The secret one. The missing one.

My heart feel like it's trying to escape my chest as I lay the book on the small table before me. Someone snuck into the house in the chaos. They found the book on the desk where I left it. They stole away with it. And somehow, I didn't hear that happen despite the fact that I was only a few strides away from the desk, locked in the closet.

I suck in a long, gasping breath.

"Drink with me, Ilsaletta Redtide."

Princess Jendaya sets a porcelain teacup and saucer in my hand. It is delicate and finely wrought – far too fine for Saltfast. It should be an honor to be served by the princess's own hands. It feels like a death sentence. My hand shakes, sloshing hot tea across my wrist.

I don't want to sip the tea, but when Jendaya brings her cup up to her lips she pauses, watching me until I do. It tastes of clover flower. It's just like the tea I drank on my birthday.

"You have my father's book," I say carefully. I don't know why I'm telling her that I know. It's obvious that I won't be going anywhere with these guards on either side of me. They're probably just toying with me while the man who hammers metal rings into the wall gets ready to install some for me. But I want any information I can get.

"Admiral Redtide always struck me as a loyal man," Princess Jendaya flips a long ringlet over her shoulder, regarding me with hooded eyes.

"He is loyal to the crown," I agree. My eyes are set on the book. I must have it back. I don't understand everything written within it, but my father is not an idle man. He does not do things for no reason. He would not have kept this book or scrawled in the last few pages of it if it wasn't valuable – maybe even enormously valuable.

"I think we will see how loyal he is," Jendaya says sweetly. "We will send him a letter with a lock of your hair and see what he says to that. Do you think he is so loyal to you that he will come to your rescue, or so loyal to the crown that he will stay away at our order?"

"I think he'll surprise you," I say through gritted teeth – because he's always surprised me and why should he do any differently for her?

"Very little does," she says with a tight smile. "Did he have other books like this? Perhaps a locked box that went with them?"

"No," I say, but my mouth is dry as dust. I take another sip of the tea.

"Any friends who came with strange markings on their hands?"

"His friends are all sailors. There isn't one of them who *doesn't* have markings on his hands," I say grimly. This is not going as I expected and no matter how much I shift in my chair, I know it is useless. I am surrounded. There is no way out.

She nods to one of the men towering over me and he twitches. I flinch, knowing a blow is coming, but it doesn't land. Again, my shadow catches the hand, shoving it back.

Scourges!

I stifle a gasp. I thought he was gone! I thought he'd left when I chose to save the princess.

Save her. Good joke. Tell another one. No one has joked with me in a long time.

I clench my jaw as hard as I can and try to keep from twitching or otherwise indicating that I can hear the shadow's voice.

"Do that again," Princess Jendaya says in a low voice.

I say nothing. I don't even flinch as the guard aims another blow at me. Instead, I snatch back my father's book as Vargaard deflects the second blow. I don't know why I want the book so much except that she does too, and I would do anything to defy her.

I have seen souls like this girl's before. They gleam like the skin of serpents and they rot like meat left in the ground.

I catch his eye as he drops the guard's arm. Something burns hot and fierce in the depths of those shadowed eyes. If he was human, I'd find that attractive. I fight against a string inside me that wants to tighten and shrink the distance between us. That's foolhardy and I'm not a fool.

I need to get out of here while I can. If Vargaard is here, maybe he can hold them off while I flee.

Yes.

I drop the teacup and dart to the window. I balance on the frame, weighing the jump I'll have to make. I can do it.

"How very interesting," Princess Jendaya says, coming to her feet. She is still sipping from her cup. "It seems that physical harm will not be effective with you."

One of her guards crumples. Vargaad releases his throat and lets him drop on the floor.

I gather my strength and prepare to leap. I'll have to land just like *that* and then twist like *this.* I see it in my mind's eye. I am ready.

Go now.

"Fortunately," the Princess says in that eerily calm voice of hers, "I always have backup plans."

Ilsaletta —

I hear a grunt, spin to see what it is, find my head is very dizzy, and then promptly fall over onto the wooden floor. It is sticky against my cheek as the light fades and the princess's dancing brown eyes are the last thing I see.

Nakuraki

Someone has snatched the sun from the sky and I am banished to darkness. It howls in pain, whistling down the pathways of my mind and I am battered with memories.

I am dying on an open field, my horse atop me. He has been pinned on top of me for the last day as I slowly breathe my last, his back broken by a war hammer. The azure sky winks at me and death calls her sweet croon.

No. That is not me. That's another man.

I am torn in two by a man who is not a man. A wolf that is not a wolf. Wicked fangs strip my sweet flesh to ribbons and I am pain and jagged ruin, panic and fear and a well of madness that never ends.

Still not me.

I have lost my light and my north star. I am adrift.

Caught between the shadow of the sword and her shadow, two dawns until the vow is complete. Does she know? Can she guess?

Will she reach into the darkness and save my soul?

Chapter Eight

I wake in manacles. My mouth feels like it's been stuffed with wool. I half expect it to be, but no – it must be the last dregs of the tea.

I sense Vargaard. He is not happy. How can I read his emotions when I can't see him?

Scourges. Scourges. Scourges.

I don't have to know why that's a curse to know it is one. It's said as vehemently as any curse I've heard after crushed fingers or ruined dinner. Maybe they had some kind of terrible dark army called the Scourges back when he was alive. Or maybe it was a disease. Or a name for something people did together – something almost vile, or all the way vile – these are usually the things curses are made of. That and the names of gods. People are always insulting what they worship as if this puts them above it.

I can confirm that it is not comfortable to have an angry soul in the back of your own. But I am not idle. My eyes scan the room. They've propped my sword up against a small table as if it is just a regular weapon they've confiscated. That is good. That they haven't recognized it despite reading my father's book is also a good sign.

No one has seen that sword – the Mercy Blade – since it was put in that ocharia box.

What is ocharia? He must not be angry with me because he answers immediately.

A magical dampener. It keeps the blade from being detected by someone able to find and detect such workings. And it protected them against finding me.

Didn't he mean that it protected *him* against being found by *them*?

I meant exactly what I said. And now, mortal girl, we are in grim trouble. What happened to you? I lost you and in that time, I died death after death.

My mind stutters over that. He what?

I died. His voice is a growl.

Does that mean he is reborn again? Because I passed out. I was drugged – I'm pretty sure of it, given the terrible taste in my mouth and how my tongue feels swollen. Was he going to die and be reborn again every time I went to sleep? That could be a problem – especially if he woke this angry every time.

No. Rest yourself, my Vali. I am not born again, nor will I be when you rest. I was simply shoved back into the darkness. It was a shock after these past hours in the light. I make my obeisance. Please accept from me my deepest of regrets. I should not have growled at you, light of my path.

Whatever that means. His moods are as fast to come and go as storms over the sea. But he is here. That's what matters. Perhaps he can get the key and unshackle me.

I can prevent physical blows, but I can touch nothing without violence. If I wish to grab the key and stab it in your captor's eyes, I might, but I may not pick it up and use it to free you. It will slip through my fingers. I am surprised your princess did not notice me when I batted her attacks away.

Maybe she can't see him. Maybe he is invisible to her. The guards certainly seemed blind to his presence.

Of course, the guards will not notice the Nakuraki in the shadow, but most of those dabbling in magic can see me.

She was only a princess. Not a wonderworker.

Do you still believe so? After she drugged your tea? After she confessed to knowing about this infection? I'd say she is no ordinary princess, but I have met many princesses and I know that most of them are like vipers in a basket.

My eyes are still sweeping across the room. For someone who has only been here a few days, the princess has gathered many trinkets and valuables from the town. I see the prized teapot belonging to the mayor's wife and the baker's coveted jade tray. It's currently host to a variety of crystal flasks containing red fluid. I am certain one contains my own blood. I feel a sore spot in my wrist and when I turn my head to look, there is a bandaged spot over one wrist. Bright silk veils are hung across the walls to brighten the room and four large chests are arranged where they can be easily accessed.

Interesting. This is not the room of someone afraid of illness. It's the room of a girl off on an adventure. One involving collecting flasks of blood.

I'm embarrassed that I've been so easily trapped. Especially now that Vargaard is crowing over me about it. And I'm surprised he's back without me drawing the blade again. That simplifies things but I don't understand what anchors him to both the sword and to me.

I just wish he'd done something to prevent all this since he clearly knows so much.

I should have done something about this, he agrees. *Instead of leaving you to your own choices, I should have stayed and continued to argue with your fool-brained, pig-headed choice to insist that if there was a princess then she needed saving rather than admit that sometimes girls are pure evil and that they leave people hanging like art on their walls.*

His irritation drips from his voice and I swallow down a wave of fear. I have angered this ancient creature. Unintentionally. Even if he's apologized, he's still angry.

I am Vargaard. I have seen many men and women both great and small rise and fall in this world. I have fought on a thousand battlefields and seen great victory and great defeat. I have danced with a thousand brown-eyed women just like your princess and I have watched them break a thousand hearts. I know *people. I know what makes them wake and sleep and bleed. I even know you, mortal girl. You ought to let me guide you.*

It sounds almost like a plea. But he'd said those other men weren't him. That he is reborn now.

Even so, be reasonable.

And what? Let him lead me to great victory or great defeat? I don't think so. Which sounds childish and arrogant. But I only get to live one life and I don't want to give up the choices in it to someone else. I want to make my own mistakes.

You've done well at that so far.

I ignore his jab.

I also want to make my own successes. And to carve my own path.

He lists all those people so callously as if they are just names in a list, just faces in a crowd, just afterthoughts. I don't want to be an afterthought.

I want my life to matter. At least to me.

There is a groan beside me, and I turn to see they have ripped the cloth out of the other prisoner's mouth. I twist to look at him and immediately wish I had not. The nausea is overwhelming. Gut twisting pain claws through my belly. Did she poison me or simply give me a drug to make me black out?

I doubt it is poison just yet. She seems fascinated by you.

The other prisoner is in his late twenties and surprisingly handsome, like the men I dream about when I stroll down the beach. He's a little more battered than they are – his wrists and ankles bleeding where the rough metal of the manacles has ripped the flesh. He's a little dirtier – his fine doublet and trousers smeared and stained. He's perhaps more beautiful than they are. My limited imagination could not have dreamed up those full lips and velvet eyes.

I would say he's the most beautiful man I could conceive of if I hadn't seen Vargaard – but they are entirely different as the black puma is different from the gleaming horse.

My heart flips so quickly when his eyes flutter open that I have to gasp to release the pressure. It's both uncomfortable and exhilarating.

Scourges save me from young women.

My face goes hot at Vargaard's comment, but I can't help it. I've lived a very quiet life and now in the space of a single day, I have met the two most beautiful men I've thought possible. It's too much for one girl to take in.

I am not a man. I am a Nakuraki.

Let me correct myself. I have met the most beautiful man I have ever seen and also one Nakuraki.

The corner of the beautiful man's mouth curls up and when you combine that with his quirked eyebrow, it's a devastating smile. As violently beautiful as Vargaard is, he is no match for the warmth and light I see in this man's smile.

"I'm the Duke of Catterrail," he drawls and at least here I must admit he cannot match Vargaard because his voice is only that of a mortal man and not a resonant shadow. "I'm not meant to be chained, but if I were, I think silver with inlaid carnelian would be a little more fitting, don't you think?"

"What are you doing here?"

He grimaces. "We were supposed to marry, though I'll never marry her now."

And just like that, the charm is gone. He's whining. Being manacled to a wall does give you the right to whine a bit, but these are his first words to me. A whine. I glance at his hands. They are soft and smooth. He does not use them for work.

Scourge save me from the spring weather blowing of young women's affections. First, he's so beautiful you can hardly breathe. Now you're finding his flaws and listing them.

Vargaard can save his judgment for another time. I am shackled to the wall with a whining duke.

"I thought you were going to save me and then you ended up manacled here, too," the duke says, and I wonder if he trains himself to looks so devastatingly sad by practicing in the mirror.

My traitor belly tumbles in spite of itself.

Tssk. And now we're back to attraction.

Am I being scolded by my own shadow?

I thought better of you than this.

He has no right lecturing me. I am trying here. *He* left as soon as I made a decision he didn't like.

And I came back.

Too late to be helpful.

I saved you from being hit with a fist. Twice. And from a knife slash. And then I died for you again and again.

I still don't understand what that means.

I will not ask you to bear it.

There isn't much to say to that. But if I listen to him now, then next time he will leave me again, but it will be worse because we'll be following his path and I'll be lost on it all by myself.

I shouldn't have done that.

Shouldn't have done what?

Don't make me say it.

If he doesn't say it, I won't trust him. I will find another way. And I will put him back in that sword where he belongs.

No. Please.

He waits. He's testing me to see if I'm resolved.

My stomach has its own ideas about testing my resolve. I

heave and only manage to hang on to the dregs in my belly with sheer willpower. Maybe clover tea isn't good on an empty stomach. Maybe Princess Jendaya made the dose too strong and it left me ill like this. Gagging while in chains is a terrible thing. I bite my lip against the artfully produced shattered hope on the duke's face and the searing judgment coming from the direction of my own shadow. I'm starting to think I'd prefer death to this feeling.

You would not. Death is a terrible cold that freezes your loves and life until you are nothing but a mote of ice in a vast emptiness. You fear being an afterthought? Death makes afterthoughts of us all.

Poetic.

I try.

I can feel him sigh mentally.

I will not leave you. You will not face this alone.

I believe him but it's not helping the despair trying to claw up my throat. I'm well and truly trapped. This is worse than the closet.

I swear it on the last hope I cherish. I feel the shake in his mental voice.

What hope can a man long past death cherish? There would be no family to return to. No lost love to embrace. No justice to set things right. No watching of your deeds unfold into fruition. Just thinking about it makes me sad.

He makes an irritated sound. He doesn't like the way my thoughts are going either.

Redemption. I want to be washed of all those lives and deeds. I want – just once – to do it right. I want to do it right this time with you.

What does he mean? It sounds vaguely as if he wants to live my life for me. I have barely had a life. I do not dare forfeit it so soon into its bloom.

This time, I won't stay silent when I should speak a warning. This time, I won't close my eyes at the wrong second and watch you snatched away from me. This time, I won't let my own passions get in the way. It is pride that destroyed me. Only humility can restore me.

He doesn't sound humble at all.

I didn't claim to have it – only to want it.

It makes me uncomfortable to think of being someone's redemption. It feels like too much. It feels like being shackled to a wall. I fight back tears that well in my eyes. It's too late for regrets. I need to work on the problem right before my eyes. It's certainly big enough to keep me occupied for a while. And I can try to be someone's redemption. As long as he doesn't leave me again.

Never. I will stick by your side like your very shadow.

Nice.

"Well?" I had almost forgotten the duke was there. His tone is laced with hurt. He must not be used to being ignored. Belatedly I realize he is waiting for my name.

"I am Ilsaletta Redtide," I say reluctantly – but what's the point in hiding my identity? My captors know who I am.

He looks impressed. "Daughter of the famed Admiral Redtide?"

I nod.

"This is good," he purrs. "And your father must have trained you suitably, yes?"

"I was taught the ancient languages and the histories," I agree.

He shakes his head dismissively. "I refer to fencing lessons, riding lessons, ship-handling lessons. Perhaps even some underhanded tricks for a favorite daughter – knife fighting? Grappling?"

"I think you've been chained to this wall for too long," I say dryly.

It is still night and my whole body longs for a bed. There is nothing restful about hanging on a wall. I should apologize to the tapestries when this is over.

"You have no special skills to rescue us with?" he says dejectedly.

"I seem to have a skill for making the wrong choices."

He scowls beautifully. "We all have that skill, or we wouldn't be here. I agreed to an arranged marriage with a princess ten years my junior and when I arrived to meet her, she threw me a party, got me very drunk, and then stole me away and brought me here."

Now, why would she do that? I have known many princesses who got a man drunk and then ran from their nuptials. I have even known one or two who kidnapped a man – but I've never known one to kidnap him only to avoid marrying him.

"Why were you going to be married, Duke Catterrail?" I ask politely.

"You can call me Stekken. If we are to die together, we might as well dispense with formalities."

"Why were you going to marry Princess Jendaya, Stekkan?"

He smiles that dreamy smile of his. "I'm next in line for the throne of Ghregoiren. It was to be an alliance of nations. Surely, you heard?"

I did not hear. My cheeks flame in response. I don't really listen to gossip, though I'll ferret out rumors about a lady and a knight from a thousand years ago with absolute enthusiasm. History interests me. Living in it does not. I have never realized why until just now.

"And now?" I ask aloud. But inside I am mulling on this new revelation. I do not want to live in history because I know what history is. It is a lot of people dying messily with no real result. It is endless misery with brief moments of heroism. And the heroes die horribly and are not remembered. Living that myself carries no appeal at all.

You try to say that like you are above it all, but I can taste the reality. You are deathly afraid.

"And now, I am desperately hoping to escape this with my life," Stekken says.

I nod. Because he's making a lot of sense. Maybe manacles do that. They make you make sense because it's hard to think stupid thoughts when you realize you might not have many thoughts left to think.

"How did you go from being about to marry a princess to being manacled to a wall?" I ask as if I'm asking him how he finished his apprenticeship as a sailor. As if it's a normal thing that people just do. As if this whole world hasn't slipped into so much insanity that I can't fathom it anymore.

My shadow huffs.

People near me always live in worlds like this. It is kill or be killed. Dominate or be dominated. Flee for your life or see that life shredded.

But if he was so used to dominating, why did he want me to run so badly?

I have become skilled at knowing my hosts. I have seen that your best course is to run.

My cheeks burn so hotly that I fear they might actually catch fire.

He looked me over, assessed what was there, and his verdict – the verdict of a bloodthirsty slayer of men who had seen the deaths of thousands at the hands of people of every shape, color, size, and gender – his verdict was that my only option was to run.

Yes.

I don't need a mirror. I know I am strawberry red.

"Please, don't blush like that," the duke says, his smile faltering slightly. I don't know what he thinks is making me blush, but he can't meet my eye. "It's not like that, I assure you. I had come for a preliminary visit. This is allowed. A chance to meet my bride before the wedding. We attended teas and dances. We had a masked ball. It's all very innocent."

"That's nice," I say, trying to make up for the fact that my face will not stop blushing.

Even a shadow bodyguard who can catch blades coming at my face and prevent knives from cutting my flesh has deemed me worthless. Just like my father had, though he did not want to admit it at the time.

"Too female for the guilds or the ships, too soft for the army or the guard, too nobly born for a trade, too learned to make a reasonable wife," had been his assessment of me. He'd left with one final word to me. "When I return, I will come with a match arranged. Best to marry you to someone who does not know."

My shadow is very silent as he absorbs my memory.

"It was at the masked ball that she stole me," Stekkan says. "I didn't think pretty girls did that kind of thing. We were flirting and she lured me into the garden with sweet kisses and salty promises." His eyes have gone dreamy. It's all I can do not to roll mine. Really. He should know better. He's next in line for the throne. "And there was someone waiting there. They put a sack over my head and put me on the back of a carriage and when the sack came off, we were riding to this coastal town at full speed and the princess was demanding I marry her right there in the coach. Of course, I refused." He looks at his wrists and now he's the one flushing. "I didn't realize that refusal meant chains. And now here we are, and I must tell you that four days of this has been far worse than any marriage could be."

I wonder about that. Especially considering the bride was going to be the person who has now put him here.

"How many of the guard are with her?" I ask pointedly.

"I don't know."

"How many of the rest of her entourage? Are there maids? Advisors?"

"I don't know."

"Does her father know she is here?"

"I –"

"Don't know," I finish for him and I sigh. "Do you know

anything that can help us?"

"I know that people fell sick almost as soon as we arrived. I felt strange myself, thought the feeling passed after a few hours. Like I might vomit, but then I never did. And I was irritable. I felt like I could do anything."

That gives me pause. It's how I feel right now. My belly turns to ice. I'm definitely going to vomit.

No, you won't. You're made of sterner stuff than that. Easy now. Easy.

I know it sounds like he's calming a farm animal, but I let him. I need this.

He is quiet for a long time and so is Stekken and when Vargaard finally breaks the silence his words shock me.

You are not an afterthought and you never shall be. You do not see it, but you are my sun now. I orbit around you. To me, you are the opposite of an afterthought. You are a bright light in the darkness. My north star. My guiding vow. And though you are new to being a sovereign, still you are mine — mortal girl though you are.

I can't express how warm that makes me feel inside. It shouldn't, and yet it feels precisely like a blanket warmed by hot bricks in the dead of winter. I clutch it to my heart and let it salve my wounds.

It was my hope to keep you utterly protected, but if you do not wish to flee and run, then we shall carve something new of your spirit, Ilsaletta. We shall carve something deadly. Something that fights back.

This, I can agree to.

But we shall do it cautiously.

I ignore that last part because it spoils everything else.

CHAPTER NINE

I am not ill for very long. I do not know why, but the fog of illness leaves as quickly as it came. Maybe it really is just the tea.

You will not get very ill while I am your protector. Your shadow is already claimed. Illness and possession may not haunt you while I do.

I am oddly comforted by this information.

The door opens and hits the wall with a bang. Reverberations shake my manacles painfully and jar my teeth. A jolt of pain smashes through my head. For a moment, all I can do is blink, processing pain and confusion and trying not to cry out.

When my vision clears, I am certain this is why Princess Jendaya has done it. Her eyes are smiling as she glides into the room even though her face is calm. Interesting. When we were children, she did not crave the pain of others so obviously.

In Kazakrattan they kill people like her immediately. The – ward sniffer? I think that's what they were called – could smell them. And at her sign, the guards would descend and when they were done the priests would bury the madwoman in five separate graves.

That seemed a little much.

It was said that if it was done any other way, there would still be many graves. But they would be for innocents.

I swallow uncomfortably thinking of that and Princess Jendaya thinks I am swallowing because of her. Her eyes fixate on my throat. She smiles now, too.

"I see that you have become acquainted," she says indulgently to us, her gesture taking in both the duke and me. She strides over to one of her chests. "I hope your conversation was profitable."

By the twist of her lips, she knows it has not been. I want to curse myself for not being more cautious. It is obvious that she has been listening to us.

She opens the chest, draws a silk scarf back from the opening, and reveals a large emerald as big around as both her fists. I don't like the light at the center of it. I don't like how it flashes. Gemstones only do that in the stories – or if they are possessed by evil.

This is not a story.

Which means it must be evil. No surprise there.

"Please," Stekken begs, his face contorting. "There's no need for this. I passed your test."

"So many failed," Jendaya says, rising from over her chest and lifting the emerald to the level of her chin. She's gazing so deeply into the emerald that I wonder if she sees something I don't see.

The duke shoots me a panicked look, but what does he expect me to do? He's ten years older than I am and stronger on top of that, and he's clearly seen this thing before. He should be the one doing something.

"It's time to see what you are made of, Ilsaletta. Perhaps hiding away has insulated you, but all must pass the test."

"That sounds ominous, Princess," I say, because now she is looking at me and it seems like she's waiting for me to say something. I'm not in the mood for games. I've seen everyone I know dead in both my home and this village. And I still feel like I might vomit.

"It's meant to sound so," she says, crossing the floor and holding the green gem before me.

I feel Vargaard reacting to it in a way that feels like a flinch and like reaching at the same time.

It's been a very long time and still, the memories that flood in are painful. I hear the screams of men stronger than me at the sight of that gem. I hear the cries for mercy – and see that none comes. The Scourge of the Stolen Heights remains the same.

I feel nothing when I look at it except surprise. It doesn't look real. It's too large. Too bright. It looks like something someone made to trick others.

"What does it do?" I ask and the Princess's smile takes on a predatory look. And I remember suddenly that Vargaard's strongest curse word is "Scourges" and he just called that thing a scourge.

A sizzle of fear crawls up my spine.

"Would you believe that this is the cause of the drama in your village? And all it took was revealing it once in the common room of this very inn. They all leaned in to look. One unveiling. One time. An entire village tested and sifted. But I had to know."

"What did you have to know?" It feels wrong to ask – but she's answering me and I can't help myself. I'm the kind of person who always has to know. I'll lose hours of sleep trying to read to the end of a book because I *must* know. I will spend days skimming through tomes searching and searching. If something is a secret, or tricky to decipher or tough to understand – well, it draws me like a moth to the flame. Everyone needs something. I need to *understand.*

"I needed to know if it happened as fast as the writings say – as that poor burbling monk claimed." Jendaya rises to the tip of her toes as she speaks, her lips parting with excitement, her cheeks flushing. She loves this. "I needed to know if it reached as fully across a population. Where better to test it than in a little seaside town when the ships are away with the southerly tradewinds and the people rarely leave to travel? We are only a few day's ride from Swordheart of Cragspear and yet almost no one crosses the mountains into this afterthought of a place. It's the perfect experiment. There's nowhere for those affected to run. Nowhere to hide. Your own great house – the only one in this place – was sealed up like a bottle that needed only a cork put in its mouth. This place can be contained. It can be studied."

"Are you …" My mouth is dry. Both from the shock of what she is saying and the shock that I haven't realized this already myself. "Are you saying that you are the one who brought the plague here? That the gem is the cause of it? That you chose Saltfast – killed everyone I've known from infancy – as part of an experiment? To see what might happen?"

I want to tear her eyes out. I want to feed them to her. It takes every scrap of will to keep my voice from shaking.

Revenge like that will leave you hollow – or worse, you will like it and it will sicken your soul.

"Why would I say that?" she asks innocently, putting the gem back into the silken wrapper and striding back to her chest to tuck it away.

But that's exactly what she's doing, isn't it? She doesn't need to say it aloud for it to be true.

If she intends to use it against her enemies, she must know how fast this spreads, so she can anticipate how people will flee and bring it to other places with them. If she lets it loose in a city that is close to other cities, the spread will ramp out of her control so quickly that she won't be able to stagger the disease. But if she takes care, if she chooses locations that are isolated, then she knows exactly how far they must be away from other inhabited places. It was four days from when you hid until Herrault attacked you. That's how long they have. About four days for it to run its way through a population. If they see no one else in that time, those who could spread it will all be dead. But if they reach out and infect more people, it will tear through the land like wildfire. Your entire kingdom could be gone in a fortnight.

There was a knock on the door.

"Come," the princess said lightly.

The only person likely to walk through the door is one of her guards. My heart jumps when I realize who it is, and I can't stop a ragged breath. The princess notices and smirks.

Chalcion Faraday, Lord General of the armies of Cragspear is a face I know. He has visited Salt House and sat drinking with my father and telling the kinds of stories soldiers tell and sharing the worried glances that men of power share. He does not look at me. It seems to require extra effort not to. The tiny flicker of hope that swelled in me at the sight of his face is snatched away.

Watch and listen. Where power concentrates, so do lies, but so also does information.

"Princess," he says with a bow. There's something odd about how he moves. It's too jerky. A little too fast. Like he's forgotten how to move his own body. "My lieutenants tell me we near readiness to go. Every building of the town has been searched and survivors dispatched. We will light the flames as we go, and erase from memory what has happened here. Your surviving maid awaits outside the door to pack your things and when she is done, my men will bring them down and secure these prisoners."

"Am I to be a prisoner forever then?" The duke's voice is gruff with emotion. I flinch at the note of a whine in his voice. I hope I do not sound like that, but I fear I might if I am kept as long as he has been. I already feel like I am breaking apart.

You are not. You have had a bad shock. Your world is not what you thought. You are not breaking. You are adapting. It feels much the same but it is only a shift that will make you able to bear what comes next.

I cling to those thoughts and I watch. I think I see green mist swirling lightly around the general's face and hands. Something winks at me like a firefly in the light and then it is gone. He is not a mage or a jinn of legend.

Which means we have seen this now a second time. How interesting. Remember the pink mist around your other attacker? And now green around this one. They are possessed.

"You refused to marry me, Duke Catterrail," Princess Jendaya says lightly, tapping her lips with a beringed finger. "Even when I was so kind as to bestow upon you one of my maidenly kisses."

The duke smirks. He's trying to be charming. It's hard to be charming when you're stained and rumpled and pulled spread-eagle across a wall. "Maidenly, princess? There were knowledge and skill behind that kiss. You are no maiden, I'd wager."

It's the wrong choice. Her face shuts like a slammed door, she takes two strides forward and when she lifts her hand to slap him – that's when I see it. Azure mist with little flickers of light in it – and a slight swirl of something that looks like fairy dust in her eyes.

I expect her slap to ring out and pink his cheek. I don't expect it to knock him to the side and nearly tear the rings from the wall as they try to hold him. His cheek is split along the bone, blood running down from it.

I can't help the gasp in my throat. My vision clouds as fear claws up my throat. I will be next. I will be next.

Stop panicking. You will not be next.

I pull myself together. I have protection the duke does not have. Guilt floods across my soul, fat and inky. I can't save him with my protection.

Well, you could …

Wait. What?

Well, I can reach that far. You're pretty close to him. I could stop her blows.

Then why hadn't he? There's a roar in my ears. I think it's my heart, but it might be my thoughts. They are jumbled and I can't sift them apart.

I won't tip your hand when surprise is your only advantage. Not unless you ask me to.

The princess wipes her hand on a lacey handkerchief and lets it drop to the floor. "We will speak further when we have left this rotting hole. But know this, you suit me as a hostage as well as you do a husband. I may yet marry you – but you will beg for it first."

She leaves without ceremony and without a word to me, and

the general follows. When he steals a tiny glance back at me, I give him my best death glare. I do not want to die, but if I do, I want to die defiant.

Yes. We will make a warrior out of you yet.

And then we are alone again.

As terrifying as our captors are, being left leaves me just as frightened. What if they light the building aflame while we are in it? What if they decide to leave us here? I am not used to weighing these things. The possibilities feel overwhelming.

"I expected a cold marriage, but not one with so much violence," the duke says, his words blurring together through lips swollen from her blow. "I think my charms are wasted on her."

I can't help the hysterical laugh that bubbles up at his words.

"You'll need to find a new weapon," I tell him, but I don't know if either of us has time for that.

NAKURAKI

The Scourge. My old enemy.

Memories crash through me like knives. I have seen this come and pass more than once before. The memories tangle and shatter again. I grasp at them, desperate for clues and they slash me – shards of broken glass in my clutching fists.

I will force them to show me what I must know.

For *her*.

She still glows like the sun at dawn, stretching across the soil, caressing its every dip and mound – and now she is warmth, too. Resting in her shadow is sitting by a harvest blaze. It's bathing in the sun at Summerheight.

And yet she is mortal. A soft human, delicate as a cherry blossom. My shoulders must be a bulwark for her against this storm. My feet must guide her through safely. This is why I have been reborn. Not to worship a goddess, but to lay myself under the feet of a maiden that she may walk on my back, kept pristine from the burning coals below.

I push away the thoughts that spring unbidden to my mind. Thoughts of embracing her, of holding her close, of smoothing her hair back from her worried face. These things are not for me.

Mortal though she is, she remains as untouchable as a goddess, as distant as a star. I dare not allow myself the luxury of wishing otherwise. I will revel in the ache of denial and bathe myself in pools of adoration.

I go back to grasping at shattered glass.

Chapter Ten

This may be our only chance. Be ready.

Vargaard sounds like a dog waiting for a walk as the maid comes in. She bustles to one side, carefully packing her mistress's things and carefully not looking at us. She has a swirl of something around her – some tiny scraps of colored mist. So, that means that even one of the princess's maids was evil enough for the possession.

Evil does not care about social class.

But what kind of spirit would agree to haunt a maid and still do maid tasks? If I was a ravening spirit, I'd want to go out and have some fun.

Oh, she will. The spirit is merely biding its time. It knows that if it works with the rest, it will get the chance it wants at freedom.

How does he know these things?

I have seen this all before. I have heard the last words of more avatars than you can count.

I can count very high.

Is that a mental sniff I hear?

Be ready. We must wait for the perfect moment.

I hope she doesn't pack the sword. I'm worried about it. It's my connection to Vargaard and he is … well, I can't escape without him.

"Dear lady," the duke says, his voice rough with pain. "Will you aid me in my time of affliction?"

I think he's talking to me, but no, he's speaking to the maid. She doesn't even look up. Her movements are practiced and fast. Almost too fast. I can't tell if that's because she's in a hurry or because she is possessed by an avatar, but I can tell by how she won't look at us that she is set on her path. Whether she knew this was coming or not, she is still her mistress's loyal servant.

"I beg of you," the duke says. "If you free me, I shall take you to my home in Ghregoiren and lavish you with riches and a title."

She ignores him and then she leaves. Everything is in the chests again and ready to go – my sword leans against the chest nearest the window. And my heart is pounding because soon the guards will return and for at least a moment they will need to remove our manacles from the wall so they can take us with them – if they are taking us with them.

Take no food or drink from their hands.

I'll never drink clover tea again.

The duke turns to me now. "I know you will be free, dear Ilsaletta. When you are, please take me with you."

I frown at him. He should be quiet so we can hear approaching footsteps.

"It didn't work on the maid, so now you're trying it on me? Do you not see that I am a captive, too?"

"I beg of you, fair lady." His big liquid eyes turn to me. I can see how this look might have melted hearts in his past, but I have a bit more on my mind than what dress to wear and whether I can trust the charming duke with my virtue.

"Could you be quiet?" I hiss.

"Please, reach deep into your womanly heart."

I could shut him up for you. I could choke him into unconsciousness.

That might kill him.

Which would be no loss to the world.

Harsh. Don't kill the duke.

"Please! Find your way to compassion. Remember your servant, Duke Stekkan."

I sigh. But there's only one way to get him to stop.

"Yes," I say. "Of course, I won't forget you."

"And you will free me?"

I roll my eyes. "If I can. Now, would you please be quiet?"

He relents, finally sinking into silence as a pair of guards saunter into the room and lift the first chest between them. The mist swirls around them are thick and the lights that flash inside seem chaotic.

I have a memory about that. About those who cannot survive the possession. It melts their minds like butter on a hot stove. It leaves them gibbering shells, controlled only by the avatar.

I shudder. How many of them will end up with melted minds.

Around half, I think. My memory of that is distinct.

I'm not sure I want to know why.

Another pair of guards come for a second chest. My heart is in my throat. They will be here for us soon. And what if they take the sword first? Will I lose Vargaard if it is too far away?

The duke is looking at me with wide eyes and head jabs that seem to be trying to get my attention. I ignore him studiously. He's going to blow any chance at all of surprise.

You should have let me kill him. I could crunch his bones in the shadows and none would know. I could slurp down his soul like a thick soup.

I try not to gag. I am deeply unsettled by those words.

I am an unsettling person.

Those words do not seem human.

I am not entirely human.

I had forgotten that. I try not to freeze at his words so that I won't offend him. I'm almost glad for them. I've been leaning into that velvety voice and letting his distinct consonants and blurred vowels roll over my thoughts like honey. Almost, I had begun to think I was attracted to my own shadow. Almost.

But his words clear my head and set me straight again. I am human. He is not. Thinking down those lines is not only ridiculous. It's distracting. I push all my foolishness aside – just in time.

Four of the Princess's Silver Guard enter the room. Two pick up the third chest and two saunter over to the duke and me. One to deal with each of us. I don't like the look of the one regarding me. As I watch, his colored smoke writhes around his neck and twists up around his head in an orange plume. The plume divides suddenly, forming three heads like howling ghouls and then he leans toward me.

"Don't move, little girl. Stay still and there will be no harm. We'll take the manacles off the rings and then bring you down to the cart below. No one needs to get hurt, hmm?"

"Although it might be more fun if they do," his companion chuckles.

My guard has the keys out. He's fumbling through the ring looking for the right one. My nerves are screaming. Come on! Come on!

Easy, easy, easy, Vargaard says in a steady chant. And even though he isn't human, it lulls me so that I can gather hold of myself.

Beside us, Stekkan is pleading with his guard, but I don't listen. I'm focused on breathing steadily. On not panicking. On being focused on just this moment like the drifting feather on the air.

The key goes into the lock of the manacle on my right hand. My hand is free. The guard reaches for a chain on his belt. He's clearly going to manacle this wrist to that chain before he unlocks anything else.

When he reaches toward you, take the key.

I don't question him. I am in the moment. I am the feather. He is the wind. I float on the wind.

The guard reaches toward my hand and I strike past his reach, snatching the keys from his belt. He looks shocked for a moment and then laughs, but I am already reaching with the key to unlock my other manacle.

Vargaard's voice in my mind sounds like a purr.

That's right. Free yourself. Focus. Do not be distracted – no matter what you hear.

It's hard not to be. I can hear the guard trying to scream, but his scream is strangled and smothered as if he is choking on his own tongue. The other guard is cursing – a note of fear in his voice – by the time my hand is free.

Duck.

I duck and reach to free one of my feet. Something *thunks* into the wood of the wall behind me and my belly flips. I glance up to see Vargaard fully materialized. He is more than shadow. His young warrior physique is picked out perfectly in the baldric and leather kilt that flicks into being, quickly replaced by trousers and a simple white shirt – but clothed or bare he is lithe and glorious – as if shadow and darkness have come alive and made a perfect man. I shake my head and force my thoughts away from that.

No, Ilsaletta, no. Not for you!

What is not for you? Only name it and I shall present it to you, star of morning.

I ignore his bold words and glance up to see the second guard lunge at Vargaard with his slightly curved sword as Vargaard throttles the first guard. The sword arcs straight toward Vargaard. Fast as a blink, the shadows that make him up shred and he rematerializes a step to the left as the sword pierces through nothing but air. His attacker stumbles forward from the momentum and trips over the other guard. That one is clutching his throat, gasping for air as a bright creature bubbles up from his smoke. Drooping, the many-headed orange ghoul pops like a soap bubble and disappears at the same moment that a pink cat-like streak leaps from the second guard, slashing toward Vargaard. A sword wreathed in shadow appears in his hand and he attacks the cat, striking again and again.

I stare, transfixed. But no. I should be freeing my foot. I shake myself and attack the lock.

Before I can unlock it, Vargaard calls to me.

Straighten!

I stand and a sword stabs into the wall where my head had just been.

A scream catches in my throat.

No time for that. Unlock your foot.

He's in front of me, looming and dangerous as my fingers fumble with the lock. The key is inside, I manage to turn it and when it clicks, I feel myself sag with relief.

No time for relief. Grab our sword!

Yes! The sword. I don't dare lose that.

I dart to the last chest and grab the sword, holding it before me like a talisman. I have it. I have it.

I spin and gasp.

Vargaard is directly behind me and the way he moves looks like a strange dance. He can't leave my shadow, so he takes a single step, flicks his sword forward, and then retreats into my shadow before arching in another direction. His sword is fast as the tongue of a viper.

The guard's sword rips through Vargaard's shadow-form and

he simply bears it, letting his shadows shred to tatters before rematerializing whole again. His eyes glow as his wrist flicks and flicks and flicks with one attack after another. The cat screams, and the man stumbles forward as the cat disappears. There's a moment where it looks like the guard is both confused and horrified – the smoke and sparks gone entirely – and then Vargaard's shadow sword plunges through his throat and he chokes, red blood pouring from his open mouth.

I'm frozen in place by the violence. My hands are shaking so hard the sword is making a rattling sound against the floorboard. I notice and lift it. It feels like it takes all my effort to keep the tip up. But my mind is fixated on the shadows. How can he disappear and reappear one minute so that his shadows are no more solid than a real shadow? He stabbed someone with a shadow sword and instead of nothing happening they choked and died at my feet? How is this possible?

The corpse gives a last wheeze. I could reach out and touch him. My stomach flips again and this time bile rises to the back of my throat.

I may never touch again. I will never wash all this death from my mind.

That is tomorrow's problem. Today's problem is staying alive. I hear feet in the hall.

I have moments to escape before there are more of them. Now that the violence has dissipated, Vargaard has lost shape again until he's only shadow and not a gorgeous half-shadow man. I take a careful breath.

"Please," the duke gasps from where he's manacled. One of his feet was freed before this started. "Don't leave me."

Do not take him with you. He will be a liability.

But I gave my word to free him. I scramble over the bodies, my vision blurry. I blink hard. Oh, I'm crying. I don't mean to, but I am.

Easy now. I am right here.

I shake off the overwhelming feeling that wants to drag me down to where I can't think straight and instead, I hurry to fit the key into the manacle.

This is madness. We have little time.

I gave my word. I will not break it.

The key turns and his hand is free.

"I thank you, blessed lady, gift of the gods."

He's babbling. I hurry to the other hand.

If you must do this, then do his hands and leave him with the key. He can unlock his own feet.

"Blessed lady, gift me your mercy," the duke says to me and I think he's praying but he's looking right at me.

"What?" I ask as the second manacle slips off.

"You slew the guards. You are the greatest warrior I have ever seen," he gasps.

Don't talk to him! There is no time.

"Take the key," I say and I shove it in his hand.

I can hear boots pounding just outside the door.

Time to go. No more delays, Ilsaletta. We have enemies to dispatch.

Chapter Eleven

Turn!

His mental voice is urgent. I turn on command, remembering to bring the tip of my sword up.

Battle, it turns out, is a blur of sights and sounds and actions even when you have a weapon and are ready for it.

Bright eyes focus on me. There are four of the enemy. They each have the colored smoke drifting out of some orifice. It goes from a pale essence to a thick thing bubbling out of them when they see me. The first of them shouts, lifting a hand from which a white smoke ghoul ripples out.

I leap to the side, heart in my throat, limbs trembling.

Not like that! I need warning.

He is ripped out of place with me, frustration in his voice. I had forgotten that his feet are anchored in my shadow. I wish there was a brighter light behind me.

We will learn to arrange that.

Vargaard solidifies, becoming more man than shadow though cords of shadow wrap around and through his body as if to remind me he is anchored in it. His ancient clothing is carefully tailored, making it easier for me to follow the movement of his arms. And this time his hair is long, rippling out in shadow tendrils as he fights. His blade is whip-fast and he dances in strikes and whirls, spins and ducks. At the end of each, his sword leaves a ribbon of red trailing behind it.

My heart pounds, but I keep my chin and blade up. They are so close I could reach out and touch them. The only thing holding them back is Vargaard's shadow form – barely thicker than a whisper – and his shadow blade that flicks and dances and laughs at danger.

A grunt and a guard falls, followed by a scream, but I don't look to see who has fallen. As Vargaard dispatches one, another has ducked under his guard and this guard's blade knocks mine aside.

I smell garlic on his breath and fear sweat on the rest of him. His face is a mask of fury.

My arms ache from the blow and my head with it. It's like it's happening to someone else. Like someone else can't lift her arms fast enough. Like someone else just had her face sprayed in angry spittle at his warcry. Like someone else feels his blade dart forward and nick her flesh – not a big cut – just enough to tell me what's coming.

A fierce growl ripples through my mind.

I know that I am dead now. That the blow he is preparing will sever me in two, but as the pain wells up and my scream with it, Vargaard leans past, his shoulder angled down. It catches the man in the chest as his arm is extending and throws him back with inhuman force. His blade is pushed off course and it tears through my dress and into the meat of my thigh, but Vargaard's push has blocked the blow and it barely bites flesh before it is pulled away.

I bite down on my tongue and force the involuntary scream to stop.

Every guard here will know now that we are escaping.

Vargaard is doing something that involves more red streaking ribbons and more flowing dance steps. I look down at my leg and press my hand to the wound. There's a lot of blood. I don't mean to, but I stumble to the side.

Vargaard curses. I must have pulled him from what he was doing.

I look up and see him standing right before me, his shadow chest heaving. Our enemies are dead at his feet.

Our eyes meet just as the solidity of his fade into shadow again and I'm reminded that in life he must have been at least as pretty as the duke – though in a way I have not encountered before.

My lips part as I gasp and his part in sympathy and then he's shadow again.

You're hurt. He sounds furious. *That was not meant to happen.*

I can't help the shocked laugh that barks from my lips. Of course, it wasn't meant to happen. Someone stabbed me.

I stumble forward, meaning to grab a scarf from the princess's chest to bind my leg.

Bar the door first. They have heard the commotion. They come.

I hurry to the door. I have to kick a man's leg out of the way to close and bar it. I try not to look at him as I do it. I know he is dead. I've seen enough death lately to know these things. But even as I try to avoid it, a cloud of white smoke puffs up and then dissipates like the last sigh of a fire choked in ash.

I hold my breath and stumble to the princess's chest to find something to bandage my leg. Does Vargaard need a bandage?

Don't be silly. Look for trousers in the princess's chest. And a lantern. There are none on the walls.

I open the chest, grab a black silk scarf, push my father's naval coat aside, hike my dress up and start to bandage my wound. It's only then that I notice the duke.

He's in the corner, hands spread across the wall, clutching it as if he hopes he can become a shadow like Vargaard and disappear.

"You," he gasps. "You, you, you."

He must be in shock.

I ignore him and reach further into the chest. There are no trousers. I did not expect any.

Lantern?

There is no lantern, but there is a flint. Beside it lies a bundle of candles. I light one candle and jam the rest in the waist of my dress under the belt. The flint goes into my belt pouch. I hold the candle as high as I can, and I'm delighted to see that it throws my shadow out on every side.

The minute we are through the door, hold that candle high and keep it up. We must fight our way out of this place. This time, no sudden movements. And don't get so afraid that you stop talking to me. I need to know what is happening so I can protect you.

I don't want to distract you.

It's a lot more distracting when you scream in pain. Speak if you have something to say.

I feel a hot flash of embarrassment.

I can hardly see him now, so it's more a sense than a real observation, but it feels like he's pausing and running a hand over his face.

Don't be embarrassed.

You have my humblest apologies. I am not skilled at this.

I am used to people knowing what my sword is and embracing it for that power. Those kinds of people are used to battle or used to bodyguards. They want power, wealth, and land. They use me to take it. I am used to being used. In every life I lived before this one, I was a candle burnt to the stub.

It is not your fault that you have stumbled onto this.

And you should not be embarrassed for being more noble – more dignified – than any of them ever were.

But it's my fault that I'm a soft girl who is not ready to save herself. I have no skills of use here. My knees shake badly and I don't care that my wound isn't very deep – it *hurts* – and I want to curl up on the bed and just keep it from hurting more.

You should not be wounded at all. It is terrible failure on my part. I beg your forgiveness most sincerely.

His mental voice is desperate and aching.

Of course, I forgive him, of course. I'm asking him to do everything and I'm not able to help at all.

I feel a whuff of relief.

"You … you …" The Duke shakes himself visibly drawing my attention again. "You killed all those men."

"Monsters," I correct. Because that is what a man full of terrible smoke and an avatar from the beyond really is. A monster.

"You killed them all – so quickly, so effortlessly." His eyes find mine and seem to cling to them. "Take me with you."

"It wasn't me," I say because I am at the core a truthful person even though I'm not sure how I'm going to explain this. It's quite clear that he can't see Vargaard. None of them can. He's my own personal, extremely attractive and violent shadow.

In my wildest dreams … well, actually, in my wildest dreams I *did* dream things like this. But there was more kissing.

Kissing?

Where can I hide my face? He was not meant to hear that!

"You were so quick," the duke says as if he didn't hear me. "And so wreathed in shadow, that I couldn't see your actions clearly. And then they were all dead."

Well, that explained the misunderstanding. I open my mouth to correct him.

Don't correct him, Vargaard urges. *Your best weapon is that no one knows I am here. Surprise is your advantage.*

He is cleaning his shadow blade. Do shadow blades need to be cleaned? I get the sense that he's smirking at that thought.

Okay. We are as ready as we will be. Ignore the flustered duke. He's just falling in love with my morning star. Hold the candle and sword high, that's right. And now you must concentrate very hard and follow my orders as they come. We are going to fight our way free and out of this town. If there is a chance of stealing a mount, we will. If there is no chance, we will leave without one. If we can recover your bag of supplies, we will. If not, it will be left here. It is absolutely key that you trust me in what comes next and do not go your own way. Do you understand?

I understood.

Take a deep breath.

I took one.

You are the floating feather. You are in this moment only.

"Umm, should I take a sword from one of these dead guards?" the Duke asks, shattering my moment.

In this *moment.* There's a note of frustration in Vargaard's soothing tone. *There is no annoying duke.*

"Hello? Are you listening?" the Duke stumbles over a corpse and flinches and then, holding his nose, reaches for a sword wedged under the dead man.

I can't help myself. I have to suppress a smile when Vargaard sighs.

Let's go.

CHAPTER TWELVE

Ask your fellow captive to open the door and then hold the candle high.

I can hear furtive sounds behind it. My heart kicks up in my chest. It feels like it might leap out entirely.

"Can you please open the door, Duke Catterrail," I ask in what is barely more than a hoarse whisper.

"I told you to call me Stekkan," he says with a friendly smile. He crosses to the door and lifts the bar. The sword he's taken is red with blood. It must be the one that stabbed me.

I try not to think of the twinge in my leg.

I am the feather.

The moment the bar lifts the door is smashed open. Stekkan flies into the wall with a startled cry.

Two of the princess's guards fill the door and they're ready for us. Determination fills their faces. Their weapons are braced in front of them – one with a pike and the other with a long sword. I don't think they'll be able to move those very quickly, but they seem more intent on driving us back like unruly farm animals. Until their eyes land on the carnage inside.

I've been avoiding looking, avoiding smelling, avoiding thinking about what my toes are catching on.

I hold the candle high and note how the dancing flame flickers over the horror on the guards' faces. Both of them have faint traces of smoke around their faces.

Vargaard coalesces, solidifies, and then darts forward, dancing with the flicker of the candle as if he is the dance partner of the light and they both know the steps.

My breath is caught in my chest, but I know that with the candle high, there is a pool of shadow around me – more than enough room to maneuver. Vargaard darts under the guard of the man with the sword while his eyes are fixed in horror on his fallen comrades. A silky brown mist wreathes the man's torso – it chitters like a squirrel before lunging at Vargaard. I haven't seen my protector flinch before, but he flinches now, his shadow sword flicking out to the smoke first before clashing against his opponent's blade.

I flinch from the sound but there's no time for being squeamish.

Forward with care. I need room to move.

I take a wavering step. Beside me, the duke groans, but I must not let that distract me. The man with the pike is distracted by the cry of his companion.

Slide forward across the ground on one knee, sword up – now!

I obey without question.

I throw myself to my knee, ignore the sharp burst of pain through my wounded thigh.

Keep your sword up! Keep it up! I'm pleading with myself.

I can see how this is going to go and I want to close my eyes. I don't want to see.

I drop under the pike and slide forward. The sword I'm keeping high slips ahead of me and the force of all my weight sinks it into the stomach of the distracted guard.

He looks down in horror. My eyes meet his.

This is wrong.

This is evil.

It's more evil to let them just kill you!

But they were only trying to capture me.

Pull the sword out.

I don't want to. I've heard war stories. I know what happens next.

Pull it out. His mental voice is firm. Beside me, the man with the sword goes down, spasming on the floor.

I still haven't broken eye contact with the pike man. I pull on the sword but he reaches down and grips the blade. We both know what will happen when it comes out. The look in his eye pleads with me.

Now, mortal girl!

I gasp a sob, but I pull myself to my feet, and relentlessly, I pull with all my might. I try not to look. I don't want to see.

Then don't look. Forward. Now.

I step past the guard's falling body, choking down a sob.

Keep that candle up!

My arm is shaking as I lift it high again. Vargaard sprints down the hall as far as the shadow will go.

Faster! Run!

I run. I know people are shouting but it feels a long way off. I know I should be concentrating, but my vision is veiled with tears and my own gasping breaths are choking me down.

I did that. Me. I killed that man. I left him with his guts out of his body in a hallway. Me.

Listen. You can't let that choke you up right now. We all do things we need to do to survive. You killed the men in your house. Now you have killed this man. What other option do you have?

I'd hoped there would be one this time. I'd hoped I'd be better. I should never have come to rescue the princess.

No, you should not have.

I should have just left town.

Yes.

I will regret this all my life.

Be reasonable. It was him or you. No point in regretting that it wasn't you. Do you really want to be in his place?

Behind me, I hear the duke gasp. I check over my shoulder to see him stumbling along the corridor, his canary yellow jacket and shirt hang open, exposing his flawless skin and musculature. And yet he hasn't killed anyone.

Those hands of his are innocent.

You don't want to be him. He found himself trapped with a young woman ten years his junior and his instinct was not to save her but to save himself. Gutless. Worthless. Use – ah, here are the servants' stairs. Stay behind me.

That won't be a problem. I can hear more voices below. I don't want to pull my sword out of anyone else's guts.

Hopefully, this exits into the kitchen. We can rush through, try to kill as few as possible, and make a break for the horses.

They'll be guarded, though.

We've caused a stir. Perhaps it has distracted them. You're keeping up.

He sounds happy about that.

You're fit enough despite looking soft. We can work with that. Don't worry. Everyone starts soft. And all of us learn to do what we must.

I'm not sure I want to, but now is no time to object.

We reach the bottom of the stairs and he charges out as far as the shadow goes. I can almost see it catch his feet and anchor him. I rush to catch up, but a fire burns in the kitchen hearth and it is brighter than my candle. My shadow barely clings to a rim around my feet and it makes a long tail behind me. I must walk practically on Vargaard's heels.

It's hard to see through his shadow-form, but I make out a pair of guards and an astonished princess. My father's book is in her hands. The guards freeze in surprise, but she lifts a hand and azure mist swirls out of her palm, gathering to form a massive horse with a horn in the center of its head. She looks both surprised and pleased when it surfaces.

I hear my gasp at the same time that I notice her wicked grin.

"A few dead are worth it for gifts such as these, don't you think, Ilsaletta?" she says and her horse charges forward, head down, horn leveled at me.

Left! Jump!

I jump to the left without thinking. That's closer to the door. I feel something rush by. It makes my hair swirl behind me and my skin feels like it's been too close to the fire. I hiss, but the horse is not done. It rears up and paws the air, whinnying.

Out. Out the door. Fast.

I hurtle toward the kitchen door and almost crash into a guard hurrying in.

Run right into him. Don't stop.

There's a yelp behind me but I don't turn. I don't question this ridiculous advice. If I do nothing, I'll be skewered on that terrible horn.

Someone screams from behind me, loud and fierce at the same moment that I smack into the guard. He's still tugging at his belt. He hasn't had time to draw his weapon. Vargaard's advice makes a lot of sense now.

The air slams out my chest and I'm gasping, but the guard staggers back and into the door frame.

Turn.

I twist away from the surprised guard and barrel out into the street. I wish I could take back my father's book. I wish I could make sure no one is following me. I wish a lot of things.

I realize with a start that I've dropped the candle, but the moon is bright and my shadow trails behind me as I run across the blue ground.

Hooves beat the ground behind me and I smell fresh earth. A scream pierces the air.

I don't look. I am the feather.

My feet pound on the hard-packed dirt.

I've got your back. I shall keep it safe as the Halls of Felranna.

A horse whinnies from the stable and then another, and then the door bursts open and a man plunges out. He's astride the horse, torch held above his head. Three others ride behind him. One of them shouts, pointing at me.

I dodge to the side as Vargarrd rushes up in my wake and pulls the lead man down from his horse. But I don't watch to see what happens next.

Another horse is rushing straight toward me. I try to dodge but something comes out of the dark and smacks me.

I spin through the air and lose all sense of direction.

This is where I die.

But I'm not dead. I'm facedown on the dirt breathing hard. I don't even feel pain.

That's war fever. You've got it bad. Get on your feet.

I scramble up just as a third horse nearly bowls me over. It doesn't succeed. Vargaard is there. He snatches the reins and yanks the horse's head so far that it must turn to the side. Its eyes roll and its feet stomp wildly. Something snaps like a dry twig.

How powerful is Vargaard?

I bear the power of a thousand spilled lives.

I have no idea what that means.

The rider's mouth forms a horrified "o" as he loses his seat and plummets to the ground.
I guess it means strong enough to stop a horse. I move toward the horse but Vargaard stops me.

The worth of a good horse's soul is more than the worth of these men, but I fear this one will not be ridden again. I broke his leg in the fight.

I gasp in horror but Vargaard moves and in a quick motion, he breaks the horse's neck before darting up and leaping between me and the last of the horsemen. How powerful must he be to break a horse's neck? Is he getting stronger? He had trouble with those first guards and now he's killing horses.

I told you it would take time for me to adjust. I am new again. My form is new with me – a frsh puzzle to solve and master.

I am quivering with fear, but I don't scream when he rips this third rider from the back of his horse. The horse rears, moving out of Vargaard's reach. He's busy anyway, quelling the rider. I sheathe my sword and take a step forward.

My heart is in my throat. My courage shivering in a dark part of my brain. But I know I need a horse. And this black gelding is strong and already saddled. His eyes roll as his front hooves crash back to the ground, but I grab his bridle and hang on even when he tries to bite me. It's my weight that keeps his head down, though his rear legs buck and snap back in a double kick.

"Easy," I coo to him, trying to imitate the voice my father used to use when I had a nightmare. "Easy now. We must run, but you must be easy. I will be a better rider than these demons."

I don't know if I'm lying. But I need a horse.

"Easy," this time I try to imitate Vargaards liquid syllables. It seems to work.

The horse stills enough that I can launch myself into the saddle. I grip the saddle horn immediately, knowing he will buck. He does. My teeth rattle, and fear makes my thoughts skitter across my brain like water across a hot skillet. I am not experienced in dealing with untamed horses. I've never been bucked before.

Just the one I would have picked, Vargaard says wryly from right behind me. *The deadly murderous horse who wants you torn to pieces.*

The horse has danced so that now my shadow is behind me again. He leans over my shoulder from where he sits the horse behind me. I don't want to look down. I can feel my horse's footsteps are uneven and I don't want to know why.

"He was already saddled," I say through gritted teeth, and I'm rewarded with Vargaard's low laugh.

We won't be able to get your abandoned bag. I apologize.

Understandable. I can only hope the saddlebags are full of something useful. And at least I have the sword.

The horse quiets enough that I settle in my seat and finally look up. People rush toward us from the inn, holding weapons and shouting. At their center are Princess Jendaya and her ridiculous aqua horse.

They're called unicorns. I rode one once in the battle of Jer'shaii. Terrible creatures. Mine bit me.

Our battle outside the stables has only taken moments. My enemies are right on my heels. And so is someone in a canary coat. He's caught the other horse and is leaping into the saddle.

He's not my problem.

I could kill him, too.

He is not my enemy, either. Just another poor soul trying to escape.

He'll be trouble. Mark my words.

I kick the horse in the sides and lean low over the saddle horn. The only way out of the courtyard is through the people congregating on the other side of it. If I don't go now, there will be even more.

Draw your sword!

But I can't do that while I'm holding onto the saddle horn for dear life.

Draw it! I am stuck in front of you. This angle is too awkward for me to help.

They are right in front of me. I can barely breathe. I meet the princess's eyes as she lifts a hand and her terrible unicorn rushes toward us. Is this what jousting was like when the knights used to do it in my father's youth? I feel like the unicorn was born of those dreams. He is horse and lance all in one.

I'm going to be skewered by his sparkling horn.

But I clench my teeth and ride, listening to my gelding's hooves ripping up the stableyard. He'd better be well shod or we're going to lose one.

At the last second, Vargaard leaps at the Unicorn and grabs its horn, swinging from it like it is a crossbar.

I shriek.

The unicorn shrieks, too, spinning to its knees and then scrambling up again. Vargaard seems to stretch for a moment and then snap back into place beside me. We're galloping in between people now. Bodies dodge out of the way and others stumble and are pummeled by hooves. I'm going to be sick. I lean to the side at the same moment that Princess Jendaya's eyes meet mine. She's within reach of me, holding onto my father's book, her eyes wide as saucers, but that isn't greed in their depths. It's hunger. Instead of being ill, I reach out a hand and snatch the book from her shocked arms.

I'm grinning with triumph when something hits me in the back.

I feel like I've been punched. And then my right leg goes numb. I clutch the book to my chest.

Can't lose it. Can't lose it.

Pain like fire roars through me and an ache that makes me want to loosen my bowels fills my lower back. My head swims and I clutch the saddle horn as my shadow whispers in my ear.

Don't black out. Keep your mind focused. Don't give up on me, Ilsaletta. I am your Nakuraki. I will bear you through. Only trust me. Trust me.

I risk a glance behind me. My enemies bubble and run like ants emerging from a nest. The unicorn is right behind us and riding between him and me, is another horse with a wild-eyed man on the back of it, his canary doublet flapping in the wind.

It feels like we ride for hours like that with my shadow whispering to me to hold on and me barely conscious, clinging to the horse and the book and guiding the horse with my knees to the road that leads west of here and up into the mountains. I don't know why I choose that road. I don't remember making a choice. I'm just running from the hoof falls and shouting behind us and they never seem to get any quieter until the world turns the dark garnet color of dried blood and I can't see anymore. I collapse into the darkness.

Chapter Thirteen

I remember comforting sounds and a voice that clings to me and won't let me go.

Hold on, mortal girl. Hold on. I will see you safe whatever it takes.

Pain shoots through me, trying to jam its needles into my every nerve.

Easy now. I have seen worse. I have seen much worse. You can live through this if you just hold on.

My book. I need the book.

I will keep it close to you.

But he can't. He's not corporeal unless he is violent and I don't want him to destroy the book. I don't want him to destroy me.

I have you in my arms, mortal girl. Hold on.

I can almost feel the edges of arms around me. But that's silly, I know he is nothing more than voice and shadow, a spirit that was once a man.

Once? You insult me, Star of Morning. You wither my heart, Queen of Tomes. Sleep now, you have not the energy to spare for insults.

I sleep as I am told. Every order he's given me up until now has been a good one. I don't plan to start ignoring them now.

I wake to a pair of bright brown eyes edged in eyelashes as thick as an Azulean princess's and the familiar scent of smoke. The duke.

The nicker of a nearby horse doesn't sound panicked or half-dead so that's a good thing.

I blink at the same moment that soft lips crash down on mine. I gasp and seal my own lips tightly together. What is he doing? I push against him, weak and worried. What have I said in my sleep that has led to this? My protest only seems to increase his ardor.

Split-pants Snake. Child of a mammal. Creature of the Orvalian Desert.

Vargaard is cursing and I feel him coalescing. He's going to do that thing where he buries someone in five graves. I just know it.

Don't, Vargaard! Don't kill him! He is only kissing me.

My first kiss.

And it was stolen by this fool of a man who is moaning over my locked lips as if I have satisfied him. I shiver and shove him away.

Firsts are overrated. Best is what matters.

The duke pulls back, his pretty lips parting slightly and a look of surprise on his face. He's rumpled and battered, one of his cheeks scraped raw, one of his eyes puffy and the flesh on that cheek split from where the princess hit him, and his doublet torn and stained.

I don't think I did that to him.

"What do you think you are doing?" I ask, wiping my mouth hastily with the back of my sleeve. This improves nothing. My sleeve is dirty and horse hairs cling to my wet lips. I scrub them again with a cleaner area of sleeve to dull the effect.

I'm in pain – searing, agonizing pain, and yet here I am, cleaning my mouth. I gust out what might be a laugh and give up. I am out of energy to clean my mouth.

You need to be still. Lie back down. Try not to move.

Vargaard seems upset. His shadow is flickering in and out and his expression is agonized whenever it coalesces. And he hasn't killed Stekkan, which probably means he can't right now.

Astute. As always.

Stekkan stares at me in horror as if he can't believe he just kissed a girl who would get horsehair all over her mouth.

He leans toward me and Vargaard darts between us, coalescing enough to look like an angry young man instead of a heavy shadow. He's right up against me with not even a breath between us.

We're in a sharp valley that goes very high on two sides and even the center of it is a steep incline. I think we've made it to the hills outside the city. This is a place for rain waters to shed. Large boulders and spindly trees are scattered in this little wedge of another world.

I take it in quickly, assessing. We should be safe here temporarily.

Our horses are picketed to one side. A fire has been lit. It's throwing just enough light to spread a shadow behind my injured body. Vargaard is wrapped forward from where he is anchored behind me, blocking the duke.

I will rip his flesh from his bones.

You will not, Vargaard.

"Your shadow magic," Stekkan says, swallowing. "It had withdrawn but now I see … I am no threat to you lady. I am no threat. I caught your horse as he plummeted forward, his rider slumped over the saddle. We fled together, you understand?"

His eyes are wide with fear.

"That doesn't explain the kissing," I say, but I'm surprisingly light-headed.

To be frank, you are in trouble. There is an arrow buried in your back. Your leather belt took the worst of it, and your father's coat helped, but the arrow is still there. You must really have hated his kiss not to be screaming about the pain in your back right now. He might need to take lessons.

You can't take lessons for kissing.

Perhaps, one day, I will prove you wrong.

I try to reach to feel my back. I'm propped on my side. Someone has put saddlebags behind my shoulders and hips so I can't turn onto my back.

This mammoth fool is not entirely unknowledgeable about wounds. He did that before he was fool enough to kiss you.

"I … I… I…" the duke is saying. I try again to feel for the arrow and slump. I am weak. Weak as a kitten. I feel a sudden stab of panic. Weak and in pain with no one to help me but this man who was useless in the fight and now is trying to kiss me.

I'm glad you noticed that. I was afraid I was going to have to point it out.

That I'm weak as a fresh-born chick?

That the duke was useless in the fight.

Again, I huff something that was meant to be laughter but is only pain-laced misery.

"You were so beautiful lying there on the ground that as I placed your cloak over you, that it reminded me of a tale I heard as a child. In the tale, love's first kiss heals a sick woman and gives her full health, and so, I thought to kiss you," the duke says, finally forming a thought. "And also you saved me from the monsters. You're a monster slayer."

"I'm a girl ten years your junior," I manage to say but now that the battle fever is wearing off and the surprise from waking in a strange place with a stranger stealing my first kiss, the pain is getting worse. My hand begins to shake.

Don't frighten him away.

Says the guardian who was threatening to kill him.

I've thought better of it. We need him to take off your clothes.

What? I see double for a moment.

I would if I could.

Would he, now? His answering flutter seems embarrassed.

My mouth is dry. I try to think of what to say to the duke. He's very, very pretty even now in his disheveled clothing, biting his full lip nervously, but I am ill with pain.

We need him to draw the arrow out for you and tend the wound. You can't do it yourself and I cannot do it either.

"I think," Stekkan says carefully, "that your level of skill and violence, your ability to slay monsters and slash our way to freedom, gives you the added ten years made up for in merit. I did not understand why you came through the window into the princess's room when you so clearly could see her for what she was – a thing I did not see until it was too late. But now I see. You came to rescue me. And you kept me safe the entire time like a guardian angel. You threw yourself into danger for my sake so that I could stumble along in your wake, safe and unharmed. You even made sure to take a rider off of a horse for me before you took one for yourself. Your selflessness, lady, knows no bounds. And so, I had planned to pledge my troth to you and with it my name and lands."

"I have an arrow in my back," I say stupidly because he's making my head spin. "Your magic kiss did not cure it."

"It is true," he says gravely. "And a poor thank you I am giving you blathering on here instead of getting it out for you. But I can do that, at least, now that we are here. I've been heating water to boiling to clean the wound. You understand?"

"I understand how cleaning works," I say tiredly and I hate myself for being so bad-tempered but I really am in pain and I don't know what to do with the duke because I didn't save him. Vargaard did. And quite accidentally.

Do you think he will propose marriage to me *if he finds out?*

I rather doubt it.

Stekkan steals a look at me from under those thick eyelashes and I think he might offer marriage to me all over again. I cringe inside.

A week ago, I might have considered it. Mostly because I'm not dead and Stekkan's sheer beauty makes my stomach flip flop. It would be impossible not to consider an offer from someone like that. Even more impossible for my father. Though we are of a good rank, we are not next in line to any throne. But I feel differently now. My old life is shattered. It isn't coming back. And thoughts of marrying pretty dukes who didn't lift a finger to fight when the blades were drawn just feels … well, it feels wrong.

"Here is the pommel of your magical sword," the duke says, edging my sword toward me. To my surprise the naked blade is lying beside me, nearly touching my hands already. "You can grip that. You'll want something to focus on while I'm working and something to do with your hands other than flail."

"Why do you know so much about wounds?" I ask, because I'm trying to be nicer to him. After all, he is about to open up my back.

His smile is kind and – impossibly – it makes him even prettier. I hate that I notice that.

This is not a romantic encounter in the forest. Or a fairy tale where love conquers all. The princess will send her men after you. From the look of that fire, we've been here about an hour as he settled you and built it, filled the pot with water and boiled it, cleaned the small knife. We have little time. And he really does seem to know leaf cutting.

What does leaf cutting have to do with anything?

Medicine? Is that the word?

Perhaps. But why doesn't Vargaard know how long we've been

here?

When you are unconscious – I am no longer here. I pop back into this world when you are back with us.

"I am not a fighting man," the duke says in his silky accent as he brings the hot water and knife over. "Here, bite this." He puts a leather bag beside me and slips the strap into my mouth. It tastes of horse. Just like my first kiss. "But, I am a well-educated man. And I spent a few years training with the crown physician when I was about your age. He taught me the basics of herbs and medicines and how to treat wounds and illnesses both small and great. We attended my father's Hack Crow Raiders after a great victory. It was a day that made me a man. I saw no victory in the shells of men we worked upon. I saw only a hundred small defeats."

And yet he still dressed in a canary coat and tried to woo a princess to marry him.

That doesn't sound bitter at all. Why can't a man know death and still embrace life? Is it so terrible?

I didn't know about terrible, but that felt impossible to me. I agree with the duke on this.

And yet you've been thinking more about his kisses than the arrow in your back.

It must not be very deep.

Try letting go of the sword pommel and say that again.

I let go and pain fills me. I can't think. I can't breathe.

Grab the sword!

I fumble over dry leaves and my hand finds leather-wrapped

steel. In gratitude, I cling to it and the pain fades to a duller version of itself.

Ah.

And now we see what magic lies in the sword without me there. A strong kind I would wager. Strong enough to siphon off your pain.

But not all of it.

To take all of it would be a disaster. Pain is important. It tells the body to slow down before it breaks something that cannot be fixed. Now, calm yourself and take deep breaths. Loverboy is about to remove your arrow.

"I'm afraid I'll have to cut your dress. There's no saving it entirely and there are no more dresses in the saddlebags. I checked," the duke is saying kindly. His hands are gentle on me. "You'll be forced into men's clothing. But that might help. We will need to go undetected when we flee here. And we'll have to flee soon."

Even I know that, but I say nothing because I'm biting down on the leather, and I think talking as he works is how he handles the intensity of this situation.

"I have to break the shaft," he says gently. "And I have to do it without moving the arrowhead or I will cause more damage. That means I need you to be very still."

I have no confidence that he can do this. After all, he screamed like a girl back there in that fight. I bite down on the leather and grip the pommel of the sword with both hands.

I don't understand why 'scream like a girl' is considered an insult. Have you been to a childbed before?

I have not.

Vaguely, I feel Stekkan positioning his hands on the shaft. Every hair of movement makes me want to scream. I feel sweat popping out along my brow.

Many women scream in childbed. Scream with such power and might that they defy pain and bring into the world vibrant new life. There is power in their screams. Strength and defiance. They show that being afraid need not conquer you and that agony is not the end but a beginning.

I'm distracted enough by his reverence that the snap takes me by surprise. I don't flinch until after. My breath comes out in a pained *wuff* around the leather strap but I keep from screaming – this time.

"Easy now, easy," the duke says, and his voice sounds a little like it's trembling, too. "The shaft is broken. I must cut the belt to ease it off the arrow. Fortunately, it is not your sword belt."

I'm not even listening. I'm shaking all over.

Your muscles are tensing against the threat. You will make it worse. You must relax them.

Relax? In the face of pain? Aren't you the one who was just going on and on about screaming?

There is a time to scream and a time to surrender. This is the time to surrender. The canary knows what he is about. He broke the shaft correctly.

I hear the fabric of my dress tear.

"I couldn't save the dress anyway," Stekkan says and his voice is soft like he's trying to lull me to sleep. "Too much blood. It's deep in the fiber and you'll never get it out now."

Just like him to worry about clothing. I stop the critique

before it gets further than that – because he built the fire and he's tending my wounds even though he knows we're being chased and just because he had no courage at the inn doesn't mean this isn't a courageous thing he's doing now.

Don't go soft on me now, book warrior.

Not soft – just thankful. I am thankful for his courage in this.

"And now I must remove the arrowhead, and this will hurt. They barb them, so it must be cut out. Fortunately, it has not penetrated deep and I think it has missed your kidney."

This pain is too much to be fully dulled. I bite my strap, grip the sword and try my hardest not to scream because even if women scream in childbed, I feel like most of them are probably not being hunted while they do it.

The duke is saying something that I can't hear over my own pained misery and the shadow is saying something, too, but I hear nothing until at long last the pain eases and I am left panting and gasping, clinging to my magic sword like a lifeline.

"It's out," are the first words I can actually hear from Stekkan. "It wasn't in deep and that is a mercy. No foul smell. I don't think it hit guts or organs. This is good."

I'm sure it is, but it feels anything but. I'm gulping down breaths of fresh air and trying not to think about how I'm going to ride like this.

Be the feather. Thinking of the future will not help right now. You are in this moment alone, drifting on the wind of time.

The feather shivers.

I think I feel Vargaard laugh at that. His laugh sends little shivers through my raw nerves and leaves me a little breathless.

Behind me, I feel Stekkan shift. "I must clean this now and stitch it. And it must be done more hastily than I'd like."

I nod because I can't speak with leather in my mouth. I am surprised by this Stekkan. He is thoughtful and knowledgeable, absorbed in his task, and not even bothering to be charming. I think he makes a better doctor than a duke. He should have stuck to that.

People think they have a choice in who they will be, but the choices are very limited, mortal girl. Born as he was, he had no more choice over his future than most dockworkers do. He will be duke or nothing. Anything else is just a dream and wish.

What if he doesn't want to be duke?

Then he can be dead. That's his other option. Surely, you realize this? You are no fool and you knew yourself that your options were the same. Your father was coming home with a husband for you. You could marry him and choose to join his life, or you could be a spinster in that tall house of your father's until he died and then likely become penniless and live a meager life alone on the edge of town begging for scraps in your twilight years.

Harsh. I flinch at Stekkan's work and he murmurs something comforting to settle me.

True. It is the same for the dockworker. If he's very lucky and wants it, then maybe a ship will take him as sailor. If he's very adventurous, perhaps he can set out on the road and move inland and find a farmer willing to take him as a hand. Or he stays on the dock forever. If he has ambitious parents, perhaps they secure him an apprenticeship as a baker or blacksmith – but that is hard come by. His options – though they are more than yours – are limited and rife with risk.

I could have set out on the road, too.

And what? Be set upon by bandits, ravaged, and killed? Live in destitution because your soft limbs are not useful for labor?

That was even harsher. I bit harder on the leather, angry because I know his words are right. I've been reading stories of kings and queens, generals and advisors all my life. I know more history than anyone other than my father. I know languages and maps. And all of that has been a distraction from the fact that I will never be a scribe or advisor. I will only be a runaway noble girl who has lost her home and place, whose father is far away, whose future dangles by a thread. My very best option might be if I can seduce the duke into marrying me.

A hysterical laugh shudders through me and Stekkan makes a soothing sound again as he draws the stitches tight. I will call the doctor part of him "Stekkan" from now on and the arrogant fool part of him "the duke." Maybe I should have accepted the duke's kiss while I had the chance.

Vargaard is growling again.

And now I'm doubly the fool because dukes do not marry girls like me. Even ones who are absurdly grateful to be alive. I am not even worthy of that. I sink into the pain of the stitches, embracing it as one thing I have the right to – my own hurts.

I have been lying to myself that I might be allowed a choice or an adventure in life. I am a fool. And I do not like being a fool.

I grit my teeth and determine that I will reject this future.

I hate to break in on a good pity feast, but do I need to be the one to point out that you have already changed your future?

Yes, I am more likely to die now.

You have made a powerful enemy – Princess Jendaya. Sometimes, the greatness of our enemies is what lifts us to be great heroes.

A great hero with a facility in languages.

Who knows how that will prove helpful? You hold a sword that is dulling your pain. That alone is valuable.

So, I am valuable for what I possess?

We all seek value in that — whether it is because we possess our own wits, or our own wills, or armies that number in the thousands. It's a human thing. And even a non-human thing.

Well, I will not find my worth in an object that can be snatched from me. Because then I can have my worth snatched away. Again. As it was when my home was destroyed and my friends were all killed.

Easy now, bitterness is best swallowed a little at a time. Too much and you will grow drunk on it.

Stekkan finishes his stitching and murmurs to me to be still while he finds something to bandage me.

Vargaard seems to pause before saying.

You could see your worthiness in me. I will not abandon you. And I can help you achieve great ends. I make you a powerful warrior even though you've never wielded a blade until now. I can make you a great assassin, or thief, or adventurer. I seem to remember making one woman a goddess.

A goddess?

Well, that's what people called her when they bowed and worshipped her. Goddess of the Shadow. Queen of Twilight. Vessuthia.

I'll pass on the goddess option, thank you.

Suit yourself. But think on it. I change the game. I change how it is rigged. Now, for the first time, you can truly choose your fate and override the limits on your choices. You can do something different.

If I survive the rest of the night.

Indeed. That will be the first step.

CHAPTER FOURTEEN

"We can't stay here," Stekkan says carefully as he finishes bandaging my wound. He's cut the edge off a blanket from the saddlebags. "It's a mercy they aren't upon us already."

"Where are we?" I ask, pulling the leather strap from my mouth. My breathing is rough when I let go of the sword, but when I hold it, I feel little pain. I'll need to ride clutching the pommel.

"That mystery, lady, is for you to unravel." He's sinking back into his duke charms. "We plummeted down the north road and then took a winding path to the west and when I saw this crevice between the hills, I pulled the horses into its shelter."

I pause, tracing what I think is the path in my mind.

I look up the steep hill filled with tumbled rocks and spindly trees and I think I know where we are.

"The Old Road should be up there," I say. "They built it on a ridge of high ground, but it was narrow and too hard to shore up, so a hundred years ago the new road was built in the lowland."

"After a hundred years, it's likely unpassable," he says with a dismissive wave and then offers me a hand up.

I can't rise with the sword in my hand. I'm too weak for that. I take his hand reluctantly and let him help me to my feet.

Breath puffs through my lungs and pain swells with it, rolling over me in red waves of searing agony. I fight against dark stars in my vision and sag against him.

"The sword," I gasp.

He reaches down for it, lifts it, and then pauses, examining it.

"There is something odd about this piece," he says, and my breath catches in my throat.

"The old road is still passable," I say, trying to draw his attention away from the sword. An hour ago, I was worried enough, fearing I would be parted from Vargaard if the sword was stolen. Now, with this wound in my back, its value is even greater. I need it if I am to face the pain coming. It's hard to speak without the sword in my hand. I feel sweat breaking across my forehead. "The trees grow very close to it and sometimes on the road, but the trail is run by game and hunters. It's still passable for horses riding single file."

"Mmmm." He isn't listening. His eyes are on the sword. "The blade says, 'Agony is an end.' Do you know what that means?"

"I know it means you can read ancient Tyrillic," I say acidly.

He turns and lifts a brow. "And so can you."

He looks older suddenly – or rather his age. Late twenties. Face shadowed in a five-day beard – though it's not all that thick. His eyes narrow as he looks at me.

"I'd like it back," I say, because the first sally in a battle should be direct unless you think you can strike secretly and win in one blow.

"It's a unique thing," he says, considering. He weighs it on his palm, his head tilting as he examines the etching in the crosspiece.

"And so am I." I don't know why I've said that. There's nothing I can do to get that blade back if he takes it.

Nothing? You can ask me for help.

But whatever I've said makes his eyes light in a hungry way and he steps closer and leans in so that his breath caresses my cheek.

I do not flinch. I will not show weakness.

"And so you are," he whispers and before I realize what he's doing, he has slid the sword into my scabbard so gently that I hear no sound.

He steps back and my hand finds the pommel of the sword. I sigh in relief, standing straighter as it siphons my pain.

And what does it do with my pain once it takes it away?

That, my mortal Vali, is the question. It is taking in so much pain – what will it do with it when it is as full as a reservoir?

"If we can walk the horses up this drainage valley, we can reach the road. It's doubtful that the princess will know about it. We'll make better time on a road and it will make it less likely that they'll just stumble on us." I speak in a rush before I second guess myself. Even with the sword, I'm not certain that I'll make it up that hill.

He tilts his head to the side and frowns, his arms crossing over his chest.

"I'll help you navigate it to the main road," I say. "I haven't been all over this side road, but I know the area a little and I'm sure I can get us back to the King's Highway."

"And?" he asks and there's an edge to his words.

"And then you can return to your home," I say. I feel lightheaded. The injury and doctoring have taken a lot out of me. I lean heavily on the pommel of my sword so that it almost pulls the sword belt down over my hips. "In safety."

His expression is pure arrogance and disdain.

Now I am frowning with him. "Is this not what you desire?"

"I was waiting for some thanks. Some word of appreciation," he says pointedly.

I feel what blood I have left rush to my cheeks. "My apologies." The words taste like dust in my mouth. "Thank you for your work in taking the arrow out and patching me up."

This man! Does he not realize that even now we are being followed? Our lives depend on the right course of action and that we do it quickly. He's too caught up in himself and his own feelings.

The duke nods, looking somewhat mollified. "I don't like the idea of asking the horses to climb this in the dark. The footing is poor."

"Do you like the idea of waiting the night out down here?" I try to keep my tone neutral but I'm not sure I succeed. I'm glad I don't have to marry the duke. I don't respect him. Who cares what a man looks like if you can't trust him to make good decisions?

After a moment, he shrugs and pours water from the small pot onto the fire. Steam flares into the darkness and it takes me a moment to blink free of afterimages so my eyes can adjust to the darkness.

We make our way slowly up the hill in near-silence. We're each holding the bridle of a horse. I am barely managing the walk even without the horse to guide. If it weren't for the sword, I'd have passed out by now, but even with it, I am still human. I still feel weak from loss of blood. Everything spins and my stomach rolls with it. I bite my lip hard and tell myself to keep going when it feels like I will fall over.

Fortunately, my horse is surefooted, and he manages to pick his way up between fallen stones as if he is part mountain goat. The duke's horse fares less well.

"For the love of – " The duke bites off his curse but he can't stop the stones his horse has knocked loose. I tense as they bounce all the way to the bottom.

We're making our way up the incline side by side rather than one before the other to avoid knocking rocks down on the person behind us. I'm glad we had the foresight to choose this plan.

My legs beg me to stop, but if I stop, I won't get up again. I take a swig of water from the horse's saddlebags, and I don't stop moving – or clutching the sword hilt.

I will make it to the old road. We'll figure out what to do next when we get there.

I'll make it. We'll get there.

The words become a mantra.

It's well into the night when we finally reach the top. In the daylight, without horses, that climb would have taken a half of a turn. I think it took us two turns. But that's only a guess. Though the moon is bright, I can't tell the time by it.

We're both puffing and exhausted by the time we reach the top, but we know we can't stop, and we can't ride in the dark, so we keep leading our horses. I motion to the correct direction and set out and Stekkan follows me without any complaint. Perhaps, he is not so bad for a noble.

Need I remind you that you are also a noble?

I do not need reminding. Were I servant, I would not be in this mess.

You would be dead with the rest of your servants.

His words leave a dull ache in my mind, but I am learning. I push aside the pain and remember the feather. I exist only in this moment, floating.

It's a good technique for moments when you must focus, but not for all the time.

What does he know? He's a shadow.

A Nakuraki, thank you. Not a shadow, though it may seem the same to you. I dwell in the shadow. Are you Salt House? Or do you merely dwell in it.

I ignore him. I am the feather. I am not blown by the winds of my sorrow or his scolding. I am only this moment, now.

I did that. For four years I did that.

I thought he couldn't remember who he had been.

It is coming back in pieces. I remember when I was a young man. They came into my village and the things they did to my mother and sisters … the things I watched, tied by the fire. I became the feather. I was the feather for four years — their prisoner before they were set on by the Sandanaras and set loose. I was the feather as I was recruited by the Istaarelle to fight in their legions.

I don't want to hear more. My own pain is enough without his, too. I am the feather.

He tries to speak again but I drown him out with a mental buzz of no thought at all. I refuse to let words into my mind. I refuse to let *him* in. I simply walk, one step after another. I, the feather, he, a shadow. And that is all we are.

Hours later, we find the old watchman's nest. I know these are interspersed along here, but I hadn't thought of them. They're built of brick and mud in rough circles about the length in diameter of two men lying end to end. I always thought they were an interesting sight. The walls are open but there are thatch roofs over them. Someone made a bench all around the short wall so that multiple people can sit or sleep there and a pit for a fire in the center. In the old, old days, watches were set there to guard the road.

"We can sleep here," I say aloud. "At least for a few hours."

"Not too dangerous for you?" the duke says icily.

I ignore him. I do not have the heart to spare for his hurt feelings or for Vargaard's agonizing tales. I have enough to bear on my own.

We tie the horses up next to a trough. Rainwater has filled it. It's likely safe. And I am too tired to object.

I snatch a blanket from the saddlebag and fall onto the bench, wrapping myself around the sword. I fall asleep like that – too exhausted and weak to worry that there is no fire, and that I don't know what Stekkan is doing, and that I don't know where my enemies are, and that I've shunned my only ally, and that I'm not sure I should have been the one to leave Salt House alive.

Actually, maybe I do think about it.

I fall asleep with tears raining down my cheeks and all I hear in my mind is a soft croon. Vargaard sings a soft lullaby. I've never heard anything quite so lovely.

Nakuraki

She is mortal, I remind myself. Mortal and very young. But I am young, too.

And if what she wants is to take this world by storm, then I will take it by storm with her. If she wishes to lay siege to the foundations of the earth, who better to bring than the one who has laid a thousand sieges and defended from just as many? If she wishes to challenge the wind to a war of wills and the sun to a staring contest, then who better to stand with her than me?

Humans are not like Nakuraki. They do not know what they worship until it's too late and they've lost that thing and suddenly they feel the hollowness of its absence. Or they worship so many things that their heart is slowly frittered away. But not so with my people. We are not ashamed of how we offer our devotion entirely and all at once. And I am not ashamed, either.

Perhaps it is not wise to have chosen this one fragile mortal as the sovereign to my sacrifice. Perhaps it is running too far and too fast, but she is the center of my world. I spin in her orbit. And I cannot feel indifferent to her anymore than I could feel indifferent to myself.

If that makes me foolish, then call me Fool.

If that means I'm taking a terrible risk, then name me Gambler.

If that means I'm risking my very soul, then bind me as Soulless and bar me from the life hereafter.

But I am resolved. This is my course. I will take no other.

Chapter Fifteen

I wake at dawn. I see the golden light seeping up through the trees. The sawtooth creepers are singing their song – much sweeter than their name. Across from me on the circular bench, the duke is sleeping with his lovely mouth open. He's just as pretty when he sleeps, which is exactly as annoying as I expected it to be.

I wonder what woke me. I lie very still, trying to determine if our pursuers are near.

But when I hear nothing, I reach down into the saddlebag that the duke has leaned against my bench and take out a waterskin, drinking deeply. I'm careful to keep a hand on the sword hilt. I know better than to think the pain will be less just because dawn has come.

I probably owe the duke an apology. He is not so bad. I bite back the wave of guilt that washes over me for snapping at him after he helped me.

But I am the feather. I will not feel that.

I feel Vargaard stir uneasily in the back of my mind, but I refuse to listen to him, still. I don't want to be scolded. Because then I'll have to apologize. And if I apologize, then I will have to feel. I never want to feel again.

I hear a sound and pause, waiting in the early blush before dawn. Have I heard something, or is it only my imagination playing tricks on me? Breath caught in my lungs, I stay very still, listening. It's only the birds and the gentle rustle of the wind.

I reach into the bag again and draw out the precious book I snatched from the princess's hands. This bears examining. I need to know why she wanted it and I need to know why my father had it. I have not read it before, but I open it now – first to the very back where I see there are blank pages. Interesting. It is not a published book, then, but a record book.

The last entry is in my father's hand.

29 Dulcast, 3rd Year of the Decade of the Great Turtle

Admiral Redtide, Kingdom of Cragspear

I have accepted the weight of carrying both the box that holds the horror and this book of history from Vaashaa Pak Shein, Gaberteen of the Farland Heights. By the grace of the most holy, may it never be opened or see the light of day.

Then his signature and that's it. No details on why he fears that it be opened.

I don't want to think about how his only wish has been broken by me. I don't want to guess what he will say when he finds out I have betrayed that hope.

I flip through the last pages of the book – the ones all written in different hands. It's a record of who the book was passed to and it traces at least a dozen languages and places through the past few hundred years. So this book hasn't followed Vargaard all his life, just the past few centuries. There's only one entry I can't read, but the rest bear firm similarities. This book has been passed with the box holding the sword. It notes who has received it and from whom and what nation they came from and the date. It's easy to commit that part to memory. It seems, that the first man listed had six other swords. This is only the record of one of them.

I flip back to the beginning of the book. My eyes are strained and tired in these first rays of dawn but reading this seems as essential as breathing. I can't look away.

The beginning of the book is all written in a single, careful hand. Someone has tried to decorate the edges of the pages in pictures of demons and strange symbols.

The book starts with a story. It is penned in ancient Tyrillic like the blade of a sword. A language, I remember, that the duke can read. It's an unusual skill to have. Can Princess Jendaya read it, too, or was the duke being held for more reasons than just his pretty face and potential as heir to his throne?

I begin to read.

This is the legend of the Nakuraki and the Seven Swords.

In the days of Sa'alui it was seen fit to bind the souls of seven Ghuhul into the blades of swords. Seven for the seven arms of the god Ta'ana. They were to be her seven blades, her seven powers sent across the earth. Tranquility, tenacity, wisdom —

My reading is interrupted by that sound again.

It's a dull thumping that sounds far away. It sounds again — another thump and something that sounds almost like a faint cry.

I stuff the book back into the saddlebag, flinching. I had to take both hands off the sword to do it and pain rips through me for a moment before I get one of them back onto the hilt. My breath is caught, shuddering, in my throat.

I hear a second cry, more distinct this time.

By now, I should know better than to be brave. I should know to flee. But the thumping is coming from further down the road we must take.

I sneak across the nest, sword in hand, and put a hand on the duke's shoulder.

His eyes open and his mouth shuts with a clash of teeth. I realize, suddenly, that it's a threatening thing to be awoken by someone with a naked sword in hand. I take a step back. Despite everything, he has the sense to stay silent. We hear the next thump together and his eyebrows shoot up.

I lift mine and step back further, adjusting the grip on my sword. It would be better to ride to investigate in case we have to flee, but the duke spread the horses' tack out across the benches last night after I went to sleep. I don't think I can saddle a horse without taking my hands off the sword – or breathe through the pain if I do. This morning, my injury feels even worse than it did before, as if it wants to be very sure that I don't forget the lesson of pain it taught me.

The thumping comes again – closer this time. Remaining here and waiting is not a good option. Whatever it is, it is headed this way and this nest is not fortified against attack.

Run. The faster the better.

It's the first intelligible thing I've heard from Vargaard since I forced him away.

Ask the duke to saddle the horses and ride away.

But to ride in the other direction means to go back toward Saltfast and our enemies.

You can leave the road at a suitable time.

I'm surprised he's speaking to me at all. I thought he was furious with me for forcing him away.

Now you're just trying to avoid making a decision. Stop distracting yourself. You must saddle the horses and flee.

I look down the road and swallow. The duke is already scrambling to gather the tack. He's come to the same conclusion as Vargaard.

But I do not agree.

I don't want to flee blindly into the unknown again. I don't want another arrow in the back.

What are you doing?

I step out of the shelter of the nest and onto the old road, sword tip held up high. I just need to see what it is. I just need to know more before I decide.

I recommend against this course of action. This is unwise.

He fought a whole inn full of guards for me last night. What makes this different?

If shadows could sigh, I thought mine would be sighing right now.

I start to walk. It's painful even with the dulling effect of the sword, but I'm so scared, so scared right to the core that every choice makes me feel hollow and shaking inside. I don't want to run any more. I don't want to be the scared girl in the closet.

Vargaard is growling in my mind and I can hear him cursing through the throaty growls.

I ignore him and set out. My shadow is long. It trails behind me like the wedding train I would have worn next year if my life had gone the way it was planned.

I peer down the flat road. It's just wide enough for a narrow cart pulled by a single horse. Despite years of disuse, no trees grow on the road and it falls steeply to either side – one side plunging into a valley where a river runs to the sea and the other side thick with trees and leafy cover. The river is swollen this time of the year.

I climb up a rise in the road, ignoring the duke shouting from behind me. I won't know what's up there until I get there and until then, I have no more information to give him, no plan, and no suggestions.

Only a foolish confidence in a sword and a shadow.

And a certain understanding that running from my fears has only brought me into progressively worse situations.

Scourges! Some fears are good, Star of the Morning. I should not have taught you the way of the feather before you were ready for it.

It's the best thing anyone has ever taught me. It means I can climb this narrow road calmly even as I hear a high-pitched scream ahead. Whatever it is, I should see it soon. I'm almost at the crown of the rise.

That's not the way of the feather. That's the loneness. You get that in young warriors who have seen too much too soon. It's a hollowness that won't let them feel. It pushes them to snap decisions, reacting rather than planning, forcing rather than negotiating. Don't let the loneness take you, my Vali.

My heart is speeding and my breath quickening but I keep my eyes level and sword tip up. I'm ready.

They say courage and foolishness look the same. And whoever says that must have looked through the eons and watched you, Ilsaletta.

I let out a long, steadying breath as I finally reach the top of the hill. I'm glad I did because it keeps me from gasping.

Ahead, the road bends slightly and through the trees I see the ruin of a wooden cart. There are no animals around it. It's the kind of enclosed cart that you can sleep in or sell wares from – or it was. It's been dragged along the road for long enough to leave a wide furrow in the earth as far as I can see.

The sides are splintered and as I watch, the monster hunched over it tears the door from the back of the cart, reaches in, and drags someone out.

It's that someone who is screaming like a pig going to slaughter. And that is exactly what this is.

The creature ahead was once a human. Pink smoke still billows around it – but it is human no more. It has split down the middle like a pea shell left too long on the vine. And emerging from this human shell is a billowy pink-smoke creature with a wide maw and teeth thicker than my fingers.

I ignore the feeling of ice in my bones.

I ignore the flaring agony in my side.

I ignore the fact that I don't know how to run carrying a razor-sharp sword – and I do it anyway. I charge toward the smoke-creature.

It makes sense now why Vargaard called the people husks. That slight glow and the smoke and the lively smoke animals had not been their final form. It was just a shell before they shed it and became – this.

Yes. Sort of. I think they have a chance to go this way or the way Princess Jendaya went. Of the two, this is not the desirable option.

It's horrifying.

Yes.

And this form is more powerful than the other husks were. It drags the human from the cart, and I see furrows where the human has tried to grab the ground with his hands and left long tears in the road.

My feet pound and the world shakes with every step. Faster, faster, faster, I force my will into my feet, my strength into the large muscles of my legs.

Agony rips through me in little bursts and my hand leaves the pommel of the sword and grips it again. Leaves and grips. Leaves and grips. It makes my legs shaky and my breathing hoarse.

Even running as fast as I can, even ignoring pain, I am not fast enough.

The human must be a priest. He wears a white cassock. The smoke creature tears into it as if trying to tear the skin off of prey to feast. It rips his cassock right down the front and plunges its maw toward the priest's exposed belly.

The priest rolls to the side, squirming.

I'm not going to be fast enough.

The curve of the road. We're coming up to it.

My breath is in my throat as the priest tries to dodge again, but the creature has one of his feet in its still-human hand and he can only spin from one pinned point – like Vargaard in my shadow.

Exactly. When you get close, overshoot your mark. Run behind the beast and around him and your shadow will pass over him so I can strike. It's dawn and shadows are long.

That makes good sense.

I'm almost upon the beast before he gets a bite in on the priest. The man howls in agony – his cries no longer have the high-pitched shriek of fear but the full-bodied roar of suffering.

Are you completely committed to this? Vargaard acts as if the priest's cries have no effect on him.

If I wasn't before, I certainly am now. I can't just walk away from this poor man. I can't just leave him to his fate.

I told you that watching the suffering of others does something to you.

And I told you that I do not want to hear about it!

I blink back a sting in my eyes. If he brings it up again, he will shatter me.

I'm too close to toppling off the edge and there is no end to the dark pit on the other side of these emotions.

The creature rears up and lifts its arms above its head, letting go of the priest's foot so it can land a powerful blow. I don't know if the priest is frozen in fear or just too hurt to move. But I do know that I won't be able to loop around the monster quickly enough – not even at full speed.

Run between the monster and his victim. Do it now.

I change directions, veering between them.

Not fast enough! Dive forward and slide!

I do what he tells me to, diving between priest and monster, and landing heavily on my belly on the other side, sword thrust ahead of me. My chin hits hard and I see stars. I know the skin is peeled from my chin and chest without having to look. Pain and a stunned misery greet me. I've lost the sword but thank the heavens it hasn't impaled me. I scramble to my knees, panic hot and acidic in the back of my throat. If I lose it … if it's gone.

But, of course, it isn't gone and when I find it I remember the stories and snatch it up quickly, turning to raise it into a guard as I find my feet.

Vargaard grunts in pain and I turn just in time to see him take a blow that sends his shadows scattering like leaves flung into the wind.

The monster swings toward me and I flinch back. Pink smoke billows in a way that feels like it is a light cloth bag over squirming bodies. And around it, soft pink light emanates.

A claw of pink mist darts toward me and I slash at it. I miss, but I manage to snag the edge of it. The monster roars, human arms slashing toward me as if it can hammer me into the ground with its fist. Maybe it can.

Vargaard is there before I can blink, materializing in front of me. He grabs the arm and diverts the swing away from me, following the momentum, and then twisting it in a way that drags the monster another step toward me.

Bellows of pain rip through the creature's throat. It snatches at Vargaard, smoke fingers long and clawed.

I strike at the creature. Its back is to me as it tries to swipe at my shadow guardian and even I can hit that broad target. I plunge the blade deep into the pink smoke cloud and to my shock, it pierces through and carries all the way to the other side as if the monster is made of nothing but tissue and smoke.

Hot smoke billows out and it seems to deflate a little before it bellows, lifting its toothy maw upward and pulling Vargaard up with it.

Vargaard hacks at the monster's shoulder but the creature is too powerful. It shakes Vargaard like a sheet on a clothesline in a stiff breeze. When he opens his hand, Vargaard sails over my head, and then in a movement that looks like something thrown while tied to a rope, he seems to hit his limit and snaps back into my shadow. He picks himself up from the ground, shaking, at the same moment that my sword finally slides free of the creature's back.

I have only just enough time to get the blade up and over me in a defensive crouch when the creature slams its fist toward me. The sword catches the blow, but it knocks me backward. I fall, landing on my backside in the wet dew, only narrowly avoiding being cut by my own sword.

My arms tremble from the blow and my head rings. With the sword out of my grasp, pain floods in, curtaining my vision with red.

Vargaard steps in front of me neatly, places his sword at the exactly correct angle, and jams it into the neck of the howling creature as it tries to land a second blow. He reels back and Vargaard twists the blade.

Pink smoke spills out onto the ground, gathering around their feet. The head and neck of the creature deflates. Vargaard steps back again and the smoke fades as if it was never there leaving only the husk of a person left behind with its soulless eyes and dead skin.

I know this man.

It's Vlorence Wavemaker, the village mayor. I've known him all my life. But he was only in one piece then.

Hysteria bubbles up in my throat and I clamp it down hard. I was trying so hard to be the feather.

It's only now that the threat is gone that I notice the priest again. He scrabbles backward. His white cassock is in a puddle around him leaving him only in short breeches and sturdy boots. He's thin and pale – with a sunken chest and a hunch to his shoulders – especially one that is scored with teeth marks, the flesh ragged and hanging from the bone.

I gag and turn to the side, recover, remember the shoulder, and gag again.

He says nothing. I hear only his panicked, ragged breathing, and little huffs of agony in between the breaths.

I try to speak and can't and he chokes on something I think might be words. Neither of us can look at the other.

Fortunately, the duke is here. I don't know how long he's been watching. He's holding the horses, but he strides right over the fallen corpse and hands the reins to me.

"If you'd hold the horses, Lady Ilsaletta," he says mildly, "I'll see to the priest's injury."

I tie the horses hastily to a nearby tree.

"I'll boil water," I manage to say. And even then, I gag again as soon as the words are out of my mouth. They are not enough to free me from the torment of replaying the last few minutes in my mind over and over and over again. I fear I will never get the pink smoke and shredded flesh out of my thoughts again.

You will, Vargaard assures me.

I step back toward the corpse. I can't help it. I want to make sure it's dead. It quivers slightly. I bring my sword tip up immediately, ready.

Vargaard makes a sound like a groan and I glance over at him and freeze. He is swaying, barely able to keep his feet. I gasp, but I recover myself in time to catch him as he begins to fall. I sink to my knees. Even if no one else can feel him, he feels heavy to me.

He's insubstantial in my arms. I can't clutch him to my chest the way I want to, and his eyes are fluttering, close to passing out.

The corpse shudders back to life and lifts its head.

Oh no.

Vargaard's sigh is deep and thrumming rolling down my spine like an avalanche. My heart drops with it.

And then he's gone.

My heart stops for a full beat before it slams back to speed.

I scramble to my feet before the corricle is on its feet. I have one chance at this while it's still regrouping. One opportunity or death.

I waste no time at all in swinging the sword. It's heavy and well balanced. It arcs easily through the air.

To my relief, it takes the monster's head off cleanly. But I'm not finished with that. I chop at what's left of the man I once knew, again, and again. and again.

He must not rise again. He must not. I must end this here.

And as I do, I reach for Vargaard with my mind, but the place where he was is hollow.

And I don't know if he's ever coming back. We fought because I didn't want the pain of his story and I turned my back on him. Would it really have been too much to listen? And now he's gone. He's gone and I feel like someone has put a second arrow in my back.

I'm hollow and flooded.

I'm insubstantial and heavy as lead.

When I finally finish chopping, there isn't enough corpse left to bother a butterfly. And still, it does not feel like enough.

Chapter Sixteen

I am making a hasty fire as Stekkan examines the priest. He has been very gracious about intentionally not noticing what I did to the corpse. He doesn't look at me until I strike the flint.

"Tell me again how you are not a monster slayer, my betrothed," he says grimly.

"I am not a monster slayer." Vargaard slew the monster and it killed him, too. A wave of panic is washing over me, and it leaves me breathless and lightheaded even when I'm holding the sword. He's gone. Gone. "And I'm also not your betrothed."

I catch a spark and blow into the little nest I've made.

"You lie," Stekkan says mildly, but there is something more behind the look in those pretty brown eyes. "Not only did you slay the monster – and I saw you do it – you heard it attacking this priest and you went running full tilt toward it. You're not just a monster slayer. You're a monster hunter. I plan to stay at your back from now on. It's the safest place for me."

His mouth turns up in one corner.

"Is that forgiveness I see in that smile?" I ask as the tiny flames lick at the sticks I've laid out. I'm lucky the forest is so dry. We seem to need to boil water a lot.

"There's nothing to forgive. You were right to take charge in the woods. Duke, I may be. Monster hunter, I am not. I will bend to your wishes in regards to terrors and walking through their territories, and I hope you will bend to mine in regard to politics and what fan to carry at the ball."

"You may choose all my fans, your grace." I give him a mock bow. It hurts and it only makes the rotten scent of decaying monster worse in my nose but it's worth the was his face twists like he wants to laugh. It seems I am forgiven and while I don't really want a companion, I also don't want more enemies.

"I think you'll be glad you promised that," he says with a smirk and then turns back to the priest. "And now, let's see to that shoulder, priest. The lady is boiling water to wash it and it's not bleeding too severely, though the wounds are deep. It will need stitching." He frowns. "A lot of stitching. But I think we can knit you back together again. I don't suppose you have more thread? I ran out stitching the monster hunter."

The priest swallows. He's very young for a priest, I realize. Not quite as old as Stekkan, though still older than me.

"In the cart," he says, and his accent has the lyrical lilt of the capital. "Everything I own was in the cart. They killed the donkey first." He chokes up here, his face crumpling. "Her screams – they broke my heart. I loved that donkey, but I cowered in the cart when the monsters came, and I did nothing to save her."

He sounds so forlorn, as if he is condemning himself to eternal punishment. Maybe in his religion, letting a donkey die is a damnable offense.

"I couldn't save cook," I say gently. "I didn't even know she was hiding in my closet."

The priest's eyes lock on mine as if finding this thing in

common has bound us. It makes me uncomfortable, but I hold his gaze the way I wish someone had held mine when I first realized what was happening.

"You live near this ancient road," he surmises.

I nod.

"Then perhaps you know what manner of monsters these are. I fear that as soon as I saw them, I hid in the cart and barred the door. It was a stout cart. It held out for two days. Only this morning, when the monster had dragged and dragged it through the night, did it finally begin to weaken so that he could rip the side slats apart."

I look at his conveyance and swallow hard. I know what it is like to hide in a tiny space fearing for your life. But I also know what this means. That he has only just now been exposed to whatever this is. I pull my gaze from his and look at Stekkan. He is realizing it, too. His face is grave and his throat bobs.

I push the pot a little closer to the fire. We need to boil this water quickly and then go.

The priest looks from one of us to the other as if he senses our exchange.

"I'm Ilsaletta Redtide," I tell the priest, hoping he won't panic if he at least knows my name.

The duke does not look up from the work of gently examining the priest's shoulder, but his posture shifts subtly as if he is putting himself between me and the priest and the movement is so like Vargaard that I almost choke.

"Redtide?" the priest moans. "Like the Admiral?"

"Mmm," I agree. I don't want to be questioned further about

that.

"I am Armend Farsheer of the Order of the Dawn. I was traveling this old road for my research."

I can't help it. I'm watching him like a hawk even as I feed the fire. I don't take my hand off the hilt of the sword, and not just because I need the pain relief. He could change at any moment and rip our throats out.

"Research?" I prompt. Because I want to keep him talking. Because I need to think about anything other than the thought that he might drop dead or turn into a monster at any time. What had Vargaard said? That some truly good people wouldn't die or change. The truly evil would turn to a corricle – a husk, a vessel of the spirits from beyond. And the rest would just drop dead. What are the odds that the priest doesn't?

I see the same thoughts reflected on the duke's face, though he can't know as much as Vargaard told me. The priest is sweating. But that might be from the wound and the stress, not illness.

"I am making maps of all the old roads before they are lost to memory. There are some maps already, of course, but they are all separate and many are unverified. It was my hope to combine them all and verify them to be true."

"I thought priests helped people," I hedge. The water is almost boiling. We can bandage him soon. And then we can decide what to do with him.

I look at the duke again – a shared look full of worry and urgency.

"Maps are very helpful. History tells us who we are. So does the land. This is a map that tells us about both history and land."

"Very practical," Stekkan murmurs.

"I was nearly finished, too," the priest says. "And then the monster attacked. He nearly grabbed me that first night. It was so dark I thought he was a man but obviously …"

His words fade away as he looks over at the corpse of the dead monster and shudders. He's sweating. Probably from the pain. His skinny shoulder is in tatters. Even when we get him stitched up he's not going to be ready to ride far and we are not safe sitting still. The princess is out there somewhere.

"He caught my back with a swipe," he says deliriously. "It hurt."

"I'll just take a look, shall I?" Stekkan says casually. But I know what he wants to see. It's what I want to see. I lean forward as he eases the priest up a little so he can look at his back. With his cassock ruined, it's easy to see the long scratch down his back.

"You don't need to tend it," the priest says with a moan. "It's only a scratch. Nnngh."

Stekkan eases him back down and now his sweaty face is pale. We need to get him stitched. He's looking terrible.

"You were scratched two days ago?" Stekkan asks.

"Yes," the priest moans.

I meet Stekkan's eyes and we both sag with relief.

"What?" the priest asks, his sharp eyes have caught our reaction. "You act as if I have just announced salvation is at hand."

"There's an illness," I say when I sense that Stekkan doesn't want to explain. "It came on our town suddenly five – no, six now – days ago. It turns people into monsters like the one who attacked your cart."

The priest yelps and Stekkan puts a hand on his chest and pushes him down.

"Don't move," he says. "You'll make the shoulder worse."

Armend looks from one of us to the other.

"If we were going to turn, we would have by now," I say to calm him. "And so would you."

He nods, closing his eyes for a breath like he's trying to get himself under control.

I maneuver the pot of boiling water off the fire and Stekkan mutters about getting thread before crossing to the wreckage of the wagon.

"About ten in a hundred of the people turn into a monster. Or at least, into a corricle – a shell that holds a monster."

"A corricle?" the priest says. He's pale from pain, but his eyes are alight with interest. "That's not for monsters. That's for souls coming back from the other side. Villains. Heroes. People of renown lost in the seas of history."

"Yes," I agree, but I gesture at the dead monster on the ground. It stinks of anise. "But wouldn't you agree that the name 'monster' seems to suit them after they're possessed?"

The priest looks grim. "Ten in a hundred?"

"Or so the person who knows this best claims. But she's only been studying this for, oh about six days. Almost all the rest get feverish and then drop dead in the first few days," I say. "So even if you aren't possessed, your odds are not good. Would you say that your order is a good one?"

"I would not serve evil," the priest says firmly.

"And are all the priests in it good? Very good? The best people you've known?"

He pauses. I guess he must be very good, or he wouldn't have survived the illness. And that includes being honest.

"Maybe one or two," he admits.

I nod. "Those are the ones who will survive. If they aren't killed by the ones who go evil. Her theory is that there are just as many of them as of the truly evil. But I think she might be overestimating on both those counts. She tends to see the world the way she wishes it was."

His eyes meet mine again and they are glassy with tears. I don't think it's the pain. I think it's gratitude I'm seeing. Not for me or the duke. This is something bigger. Perhaps he is grateful that he didn't turn. Or maybe it's something else. I don't have a lot of experience with priests. If the one from our village is still alive, I expect he's wreathed in smoke by now.

"Who were you working for, priest?" Stekkan asks, joining us again. He has thread in one hand and a hand-sewn book in the other – the maps, I would guess.

"General Fillamore and the High Priest Garason," he says.

"And did anyone else know you were on this mission?" There's a strange expression on his face that I can't read.

"I don't think it was a secret," the priest says. "Though I admit, I was so caught up in the workings of it that I didn't think to ask if anyone else knew."

"What do you see in the maps, your grace?" I ask quietly, taking the book from him.

He sets about wetting a cloth now that the water is ready and begins to bathe the priest's wounds as I flip through the book, staring intently at the maps.

"You tell me," Stekkan says in a quiet voice. "You can read ancient Tyrillic. You seem a bookish kind of a monster hunter. Tell me what you see."

And as he stitches and cleans and the priest moans, I study his maps. And as I study them, I feel myself growing paler because I see the same thing that Stekkan does. The duke, it turns out, is only a fool where women are concerned. And armed combat.

"There are five unguarded paths from the Kingdom of Cragspear to her surrounding neighbors," I say as he is setting the stitches.

"Ah, but they are old," the priest says, "And no one would be able to use them to attack us without us knowing where they are, and they are lost in time and memory. Besides, they run close to towns and cities. Someone might notice a large force trying to use the road."

"Yes," I say ominously. "It's a system of roads for getting around this country unseen and for entering other nations just as unseen – so long as you limit the size of the group using the road. It's the exact system of roads a spy network might use."

"Or a princess who wants to infect cities one at a time and eventually take that infection to other lands," the duke says grimly. "A princess like that would need allies."

"Like the military," I agree. "And the orders."

"What are you talking about?" Armend asks in a quavering voice.

The duke meets my eyes before tying off the final stitch. His eyes are still on mine when he finally speaks. "I think we need to talk, priest. About loyalties and plans."

Chapter Seventeen

We take the priest back to the nest. There's nothing in his cart worth saving beyond a fresh cassock and a blanket. I use the last of his water to clean blood spatter from my face and hands and then I change into clothing from the saddlebags. It's too loose and it's men's clothing and it makes me feel like a fool in a way my dress never did. It's like I'm trying to wear someone else's skin instead of just their clothing.

My dress is so ruined that there's no saving it. I leave it with the cart. But I put my father's naval coat back on again. The smell of him is almost gone. I have to bury my nose into the inner lining to find it. I do for one long moment and wonder if this is the last I'll ever smell of him.

It takes both of us to get the priest on a horse and he barely makes it through the ride to the nest. We set him on the bench, wrap him in a blanket, light a small fire, and make a soup with the dried food in the saddlebags and the water from the skins. We'll need more water by tomorrow. And more food in a day or two. My stomach grumbles as I consider this.

More than anything, we need a plan. And at least the duke agrees with me on that.

When we're finally all eating, his eyes meet mine.

"We could go to your country," I suggest. "Use the roads the priest mapped. Gather help."

He's already shaking his head. He speaks to me very slowly. "A lowly bard such as myself has no connections in my land that could be prevailed upon to help us."

"Bard?" I ask ironically, wondering why he's afraid to admit who he is in front of the priest.

"Surely, you noticed my bright coat," he says tightly. "I lost my lute when I was attacked, but the coat should proclaim who I am, even now."

It's not a bad cover. He makes a believable minstrel with that charming smile and those dreaming eyes. But I've been calling him 'your grace' and the priest might have noticed that.

"You could find work as a healer if you cannot play," the priest says kindly. "Your work on me was well done. I doubt I'd have better care in the temple."

His words are kind, but his face is white as a sheet and his high cheekbones jut out like cliff faces. He's not well. The wound is extensive, and he needs rest.

"Even so," the duke says with an easy manner as if what he's saying is of no consequence, "I would never want to spread this sickness further than needed. Even if we are not affected, we might be contagious somehow."

A chill rolls over me as I realize he is right. We could spread this sickness to innocent people. But how will we be able to tell if we are infectious?

"The princess will head north to the capital," I say. "And her followers will spread this no matter what happens."

"That's bad," the priest says, shaking. He is feverish and that is not good. I have no medicines for him, and we must move soon. We cannot stay where we might be discovered. "And who is this princess?"

"Princess Jendaya," I say absently.

"Oh, that can't be right," the priest says, closing his eyes. "You're mistaken."

I don't bother correcting him. He's probably only half with us and half-consumed with pain and fever.

"Which means going to the capital poses no more risk to the people there than they already face," the duke says. He's as determined as I am to think this through.

It's a harsh logic. He doesn't want to risk his people, but he'll risk mine. It makes me feel hot around my collar for a moment, but I take a deep breath. A foreign power isn't going to stop Princess Jendaya anyway. They'd want some kind of proof – which we don't have. And they'd be worried about diplomacy. They'd likely have to have a lot of meetings. And someone needs to stop her a lot quicker than that. And the only people who know what she's doing are we three. I taste acid in my mouth at the thought. There are so many people in the capital. So many who will certainly die if she spreads this there and so many who might turn and become terrible monsters.

And I'm not enough. I'm just a girl. I'm impractical and I don't have any connections. I didn't bring any money or anything I can trade for even a night's stay at an inn. Stekkan doesn't look like he's in any better shape in his torn canary coat. There might be nobles who would take me in – old friends – but that's a gamble. This whole thing is a gamble and I'm not good at gambles. I don't like them. I like sure things. I like knowing what happens next.

It's a four-day journey to the capital if you ride hard and fast. The princess will have a large group with her. And they might not be able to move particularly quickly.

"We can't let her infect the whole country," I say. It's the one thing I'm certain of. Even if I'm bad at gambling. Even if I don't want to do this.

The duke just watches me as I form my next thought.

"Which means this is a race. We either need to find her and stop her – steal her means of infecting others, because obviously there aren't enough of us to really stop her and her small army – or we need to get to the capital first, find someone who will believe what we are saying, and convince them to stop her."

"We can't race a princess with a wounded priest. He can barely stay in the saddle," the duke objects. But I can tell he's not really disagreeing. He's waiting to see how I'll solve that problem. Shouldn't he be the one solving these problems? He's the one who will rule a nation someday.

If he lives that long.

"If we go to Swordheart, I can tell the head of our order what is happening," Armend says quietly. "He knows the King."

"But he sent you to map these hidden roads," I remind him. "So they can be used against the nation."

"You don't know that," he says quietly. I can't tell if he's quiet because he's in pain or quiet because he's furious. His eyebrows are very thick and black. They're scrunched together in the middle of his forehead. "The Honored Head is a noble priest. Respected. Worthy. He would not betray me or any of us."

I don't have his confidence. That leaves only one real option – stealing the gem from the princess and putting it somewhere no one will ever again find it. My palms feel sweaty at the thought. A pang of misery rushes through me. Vargaard would know what to do. And without him, I've lost both his council and his skills. I won't be able to fight on my own. This plan is infinitely riskier without him.

I put my face in my hands.

"Perhaps if you take the gem, she won't be able to turn any more people into monsters," the duke says.

I notice that he says *you* and not *we.* I am utterly alone. I feel too hot.

"What gem?" the priest asks. I think the duke is explaining it to him. He doesn't trust the man with his real identity but apparently, he trusts him with knowing the truth about this illness and the cause.

I just feel ill. I'm going to vomit.

"The priest needs rest," I say eventually, fighting waves of nausea. "And he can't stay here in this nest. And we have to head north on this road, anyway. South only leads to Saltfast. None of us wants to go there. Perhaps we'll find a place along the way for the priest to shelter and heal."

My own wound pains me. But I clutch the sword handle and I try not to think about it. Each time I do, I think of how angry Vargaard was that I wouldn't face my sorrow and pain and that I was trying to hide them in his teaching. And each time I think of Vargaard my heart hurts.

I've grown used to him. It's only been a day and I've grown so used to him that losing him feels like losing my own arm.

"We'll have to ride slowly," Stekkan says grimly. "And I'll have to ride with him to keep him in the saddle."

He doesn't say out loud that he knows I'm too injured to support the priest. But he also doesn't say he won't do it, and there are plenty of people less noble than a duke who wouldn't offer to ride double with an injured person and tend them. Begrudgingly, I am forced to accept that Stekkan is not as bad as I originally thought.

My respect is not enough to keep me from feeling ill when he says, "What will you do, then, monster hunter?"

Without Vargaard I am no monster hunter. I'm only a girl who likes books and has a sword to help her bear pain. I grimace and say, "Let's mount up. We ride."

We douse the fire, mount the horses, and set out. It's slow going and not just because the way is winding and overgrown. The priest hisses at every jostle and when we pass the corpse that I hacked to fish bait, he begins to pray out loud – the same prayer over and over.

"All-seeing father, watch us. Protect us. Ward off evil. All-seeing father, watch us, protect us. Ward off evil. All –"

I ignore him. I am saying my own version of a prayer. It's just Vargaard's name over and over, but if he can hear me, he doesn't answer.

I can't tell how far we've come when the road begins to dip and we finally cross a creek. It's well into the afternoon and the day has worn on all of us. We dismount to rest the horses and fill our waterskins and the duke digs into the saddlebags looking for food. On the pretext of needing a personal moment, I walk out into the trees and let myself break down for a moment, crying silently into my palm, my fingers spread out over my eyes.

I can't do this.

I hear the men taking behind me because they think I cannot hear.

"A monster hunter?" the priest says. "If that's really what she is, she's a very odd choice for it. She's barely grown. She can hardly lift that sword."

"She rescued me from dozens of them," Stekkan says earnestly. "Took an arrow in the back. And you saw what she did back there. She's unstoppable."

"But we aren't." the priest says in a quavering voice. "I don't mean to be ungrateful, but if she wants to be a hero what is that to us? We're only a priest and a minstrel. We could find a quiet place and wait this out. Let heroes be the heroes."

Their voices fade. I don't care if that's what they decide. This isn't their fight. It's mine.

I walk further into the woods – far enough for silence – and collapse on my knees, sucking in a breath that's almost a sob. I'm in a small clearing and bright sunlight filters down for the first time all day, framing me in a halo of gold. I close my eyes to the sun and let it wash over me.

I know what I need to do. I need to find Jendaya. I need to sneak into her camp and take her terrifying gem. I'm terrified to do it, but there's no one else.

I just hate that I have to do it alone.

Alone?

I gasp and reel back.

Vargaard leaps from my shadow, sword braced. He spins as

if he's looking for an enemy. He's fully human-looking in this moment – propelled by his violent emotions and desires. And his face shines slightly – more beautiful than even the duke's, and more inhuman.

I feel panic rolling off him in waves.

He sees me and his lips part in what looks like relief. I gasp as he throws his shadow sword down. It vanishes in my shadow as he sinks to his knees in front of me. He reaches to cup my face with his hand, his movement oh so gentle.

I can't feel his touch. And yet I can. I feel it in my mind, as if he can touch me in places no one else can access.

Never alone again, Ilsaletta, his mind whispers to mine. *Whatever you weep over, I will weep with you.*

He's alive. He's unhurt.

I slew the monster after you disappeared. It only took one blow.

Good work, my novice warrior.

But I thought I lost you. I thought you were dead.

I heal in your shadow. But sometimes it takes time and while it mends me, I cannot manifest.

My lips part and I see his part in sympathy. He leans forward, shuddering slightly and leans his shadow forehead against mine. For the barest moment, I think he might kiss me, which is utterly crazy. He's made of shadow. If he even tried, his shadow lips would pass right through mine. But I gasp anyway and hold my breath in anticipation. It leaves a warm trail from my waiting lips and down, down through my chest and into my belly. I try to shove the desire away, but instead I feel as if I can almost taste him. I shove harder.

Our eyes are locked on each other. Our parted lips barely a breath apart. He bites his lower lip as if he is biting back what he wants to do. He's right of course, he's right, even if that bite makes me only want to taste his imprisoned lip even more.

It takes me a full minute to gain power over my lungs again and slow my racing heart, to remind myself not to be a fool over the only ally I have – an ally who is a thousand years old. I must seem like such a young idiot to him.

I close my mouth and swallow.

"Tell me the rest of your story," I whisper.

Tell me first what pains you.

"I must chase after Jendaya and take her gem so that no one else dies from it," I whisper. "But I'm afraid to do it. I'm afraid to stand up to her alone."

He nods and in that moment I'm certain that he understands. His thoughts almost stutter as he tries to form them. His hand drops from my face and I even though I can't feel the warmth of it, I miss it.

I told you about my family. About what I saw. How it broke me. I lived as the feather and in the loneness for years and I fought as a warrior in the army. And then one day, I saw it happen again.

I'm crying and I don't even know why. This is a story a thousand years old. All these people are dead, and their great grandchildren are dead.

Shh, shh now.

Go on. Don't stop.

It's a plea for healing between us. To mend what I broke.

But this time, it was not to my family. It was not me tied up in a corner unable to do anything but scream. This time it was my brothers in arms doing it to someone else's family. And I was the feather. I did nothing to stop them. I could not have – but that makes no difference.

A lump forms in my throat. I am horrified.

His eyes lower, shame making him flicker back into a man made mostly of shadow.

I bore the guilt of that for a full year. I could no longer be the feather. I had failed the innocent. I had not stood up when they needed me to stand. I was silent and deaf to their pleas.

At the end of the year, I went to the Pain Maker. And I pledged my soul to him. "I have been faithless," I told him. "Take my guilt."

The words hang in the air.

"Did he take it?" I barely recognize my own broken voice.

I don't remember. I don't even remember if this is my memory or someone else's. I just remember pain. And failure. It is not the only memory I have of failure.

Everything about this is horrible.

Justice is a horrible thing. But it is also right in the way that sunlight is right and the thick veins of rock that run through the earth are right. I am glad for my deaths. I am glad for my suffering. I have deserved every hour of torment since that day. Even if I am no longer that person.

And this is the ally I crave?

Ah, but you have the perfect ally. Because I will not let you doom your soul as I did. I will not let you fail to do the task you must do to save the innocent. It will be different this time. I have sworn this to myself.

I thought he wanted me to run away.

That was before I realized this is your death-wager. You must take it, or your soul is doomed as mine was. But I will go with you.

I'm shaking and I think it's with relief. It's still going to be hard to pull this off. I've already seen that Vargaard is not invulnerable – and I certainly am not. The arrow wound twinges painfully to remind me of this.

But I won't be alone. That, in itself, is enough to get me to my feet.

In truth, did you think I'd leave you to the tender mercies of the duke? He's a man more ready for a ballroom than a brawl.

In fairness, he was snatched from a ball in that coat.

In fairness, anyone dressed like a canary is asking to be caged.

I follow the sound of the creek back to where the others are waiting. I am not sure how I feel about my ally, knowing now how he has failed, but I know one thing – I will not have to do this alone.

Chapter Eighteen

By the time I return to the others, I have a plan. Or at least the beginnings of one.

I find them bent close together whispering.

"Let me look at your wound," Stekkan says the moment I come into the clearing.

I nod my agreement, but I reach toward Vargaard with my mind. I didn't like it when he was gone.

Still here, Ilsaletta.

"We'll find a cottage or an abandoned farm and take you there," I say to the priest. "You and Stekkan can recover and wait for the violence outside to blow past."

"And you?" the priest asks in a shaky voice. "Where will you go, monster hunter?"

Monster hunter?

It's too long a story to explain to him while I'm trying to have a conversation, so I ignore it.

"I will hunt monsters," I say grimly. "I will continue on."

"You're only a girl," the priest says gently. "I know your father by reputation. We could find a way to send word to him and my order can find you an appropriate home with other nobility where you can be kept until his return."

"And do what?" I ask.

"I don't know what young ladies do," he says, his hands stretched wide. He's clearly trying to clutch at an idea through the fog of his pain and I wonder if he sees many women in the order. "Embroidery, perhaps?"

I can't help my slight smirk. "Yes, I'll sit and embroider while the world turns into husks of humans and destroys everything alive. Do you think I'll be able to fit that on a pillow or should I try an entire tapestry?"

"Well, a, a, a, tapestry does have more potential," he stutters, his eyes wide.

I sigh. "You're barely older than I am, priest."

He nods gravely, "But I have the favor of the all-seeing father to guide me. Maybe. He tends to choose his own side in things, and I may or may not be on it. But I definitely want to be. As long as it's respectable. Which of course it will be." He sounds like a ship captain trying to convince himself to take a journey over rough seas. I almost pity him. "At any rate, I am better able to chart my course than a disordered noble girl is," he concludes.

I give him a long look. I'm pretty sure the duke is snickering behind me and trying to disguise it by making sounds of concern over my wound.

"If we wait until we feel old enough and experienced enough to face the crisis before us, we will find ourselves hopelessly mired in it," I tell him. "Youth should not stop us. It should only be a starting point."

The priest looks uncomfortable. And I don't like that. I'm not convinced that he's on our side. He doesn't want to be ripped apart by monsters but that only keeps him with us for now. At the first sign of civilization, he might bolt to pour his troubles into the first respectable ear he finds. And then we'll be betrayed. That's the problem with religion. It tries to sand down all the rough edges. And it often works. And then when you go to try to grip onto it for dear life there's nothing to catch hold of because it's been made so inoffensively smooth.

"I won't wait in a farmhouse," the duke says, lowering the back of my shirt again. He throws the bloody mess of the bandage on the ground but doesn't replace it. "I plan to cling to your back like your own shadow, monster hunter."

That spot is occupied.

"Why?" I ask Stekkan, turning so I can look into his wide brown eyes. They're meltingly warm today.

"Because the safest place in a storm is directly in the eye of it. If I stay close enough to you, I may avoid being swept up in the chaos you spin around you. I'm no warrior, but I am a man who knows women and I see the storm that you and Jendaya are cooking up together. It's going to sweep up the whole world in its fury."

"She's the one cooking up storms," I say through gritted teeth. "I'm just trying to survive them."

He smirks. But at least he seems to have given up the idea of marrying me. Now, he just wants to follow me around.

"On her own, she would make a storm, certainly. But she would make it unopposed and it would sweep through easily and be over. You plan to fight back and now the storm will rage with twice the fury. I think it will be safer in your shadow than anywhere else, so where you go, I will go. For now."

Still occupied.

"But you'll stay somewhere safe if we find a safe place for you?" I ask the priest.

He won't meet my eye.

"Priest?" I push.

"I'm trying to determine what is the right course," he says, his face twisted with concern. I want to sigh. The right course is obvious to me. It's the one where we prevent this magical malady from spreading across not just the Kingdom of Cragspear but *every kingdom* – and even Stekkan seems to realize that, but not the priest. Oh no, he must morally debate what is right in his head when it's as plain as the nose on his homely face.

Perhaps that's why he joined the priesthood. Some are celibate by choice and others have it thrust upon them.

That's unkind.

You'll find that the latter tend to take out those frustrations on others. It is a grim thing and if there is any sign of it, I will strike him down whether you will it or not.

Noted.

"Your back is healing well," Stekkan says from behind me. He keeps his voice low as if this is a secret.

I frown and he darts a glance to the priest. But Armend is still lost in a sea of worry about the moral complexity of saving the world. Carefully, Stekkan takes my hand.

He'd better not be trying something right now.

He moves it to place it against my back under my shirt. I flinch, waiting for the touch against my wound. Instead, I feel the knot of a thick scar forming. The wound is crusted over. It feels like it is a week old and not only a day.

It takes all my self-control not to show my surprise.

"You need to keep moving it as it heals so it doesn't tighten up," he says casually, as if my healing hasn't been magically accelerated. So, he really does plan to be my ally. Only that kind of loyalty would bind his tongue at this curiosity.

I nod and I concentrate on planning. I must be clever.

I know this area. I haven't traveled this particular road before, but I know of it because I grew up here and I've listened to hunters and trappers telling stories to cook in the courtyard of where they'd been getting the game and trapping the furs we buy. I've seen the sketches of the old road in my father's collection of maps and in my mind I can see those sketches right now.

I know that the old road will eventually lead out to the main road and that they cross north of Saltfast. I know it's a long haul, and people who go out here have to spend the night. What else do I know that I can use?

I'm thinking hard when I remember the cloister. There is a knot of monks up the main road. They keep a solitary cloister along the river where they tend bees and prayers with equal fervor. I'm surprised I didn't think of it, but I've never seen the cloister. You can't see it from the road. You take a little path off the main road north when you reach the bridge over the Bubblethroat River. Our driver pointed out that road the last time we drove home from Swordheart.

"I know where we can take you, priest," I say with a smile. "Have you heard of the god of the Smiling Eye?"

The priest, it turns out, has indeed heard of the god of the Smiling Eye and he is no more eager to spend time with his monks than to go with us.

"It's like they're always looking at you," he grumbles as we mount our horses again. "It's like they're judging everything you do."

I don't mention that he is describing himself, but when I glance at Stekkan he rolls his eyes dramatically and I can barely suppress the laugh that wants to bubble up.

"And will you stay with me there?" the priest asks the duke. "Will you wait until the chaos has passed and then return with me to the capital?"

"Hardly," Stekkan says wryly. "Like I've said, I'm sticking with the monster hunter. I have a feeling she will make a good song."

The priest's lips thin at that. He doesn't like what we are planning. Someone as steeped in authoritarian structure as he is must struggle with the idea of defying that authority – even if it's in the form of a princess who is going to turn the whole world into monsters.

We ride in silence after that and my mind drifts a little. It keeps showing me again what I saw and what I did to the mayor in an endless stream that I can't stop. Every time I see it again, I feel a little heavier and a little more like I want to cry.

I guarded a young boy once. He was twelve and he was forced to ascend a throne too soon. I was his guardian for but three moons before we were overwhelmed by so great a coup attempt that I could not repel them. He loved snowy owls. He had three as pets. His name was Valiant and in the times that he dreamed, he spoke of clouds full of pearls and a kingdom where all men and women were equal.

I would be honored if you would remember him.

Of course, I will.

We all have regrets. I regret that the me that was his guardian could not save him. He could not even bury him under the weeping tree with the rest of his family.

But when my thoughts are grim, I remember his smile as he stroked the feathers of his snowy owl. It's one of the strongest memories I have from the Vargaards that were before me. And I will not fail like that again. I will guard you with every scrap that I am and I will reach for all the shards of memory in the hope of finding what I must to keep you safe.

There is a sweetness in the middle of the bitter sadness that floods over me. He's already paid a thousand penances for what he's done and yet here he is pledging himself all over again to another person who will definitely die in his care one way or another. I am not immortal. There is no hope that I can be his friend forever. But at least I can be his friend for now.

Tell me about something else you loved. Tell me something that isn't death and misery.

We reach the main road while he is still telling me about a home along the sea and catching fish with his hands in the water. His words cut off as a stab of fear fills me.

I lift a hand to the others, draw my sword and walk my horse out onto the road first, heart in my throat. I have no reason to fear this place, and yet I swallow down the memory of the swollen man filled with pink smoke. There are more out there. Both rogue villagers and the ones Jendaya has conscripted into her army. But I cannot hide – because nowhere is really safe. And I cannot run – because I don't know where they will be. Which means I must fight.

It takes all my courage to click my tongue lightly and tug the rein that will turn my horse to face north up the broad road. There's no one in sight. And yet I keep silent. My tongue is glued to the roof of my mouth.

I study the road as we walk our horses up it. I can't tell how old the tracks on it are or how many people have passed by. In books, the people always know, but to me, it just looks like a road. I should have spent more time asking trappers and hunters how to track. I should have spent time with the guards learning to fight. I should have spent time preparing. But instead, I spent all my time reading books. I can't honestly regret it since it was what I wanted to do, but I'm starting to think that maybe I should have done those other things, too.

Easy now. We can't excel at everything. We each must choose a path.

The sun is sinking. We need to think about setting up a camp.

We round a corner and reach the bridge. It's so sudden that I pull up sharply, a sudden spike of fear racing down my spine. People could be near. And right now, all people are threats.

The river is swollen past its banks and the top branches of little bushes peek through the swirling waters. It's loud – loud enough that we will need to raise our voices to speak.

We've ridden in silence this whole way and the priest is drowsing in the saddle in front of the duke who looks both annoyed and impatient. We need a place to leave the priest before we all wear out.

Fortunately, the side road is apparent immediately. But it's better traveled than I expected.

Another stab of fear shoots through me. Anxiety is a worm that eats through my bones, constantly there, reminding me that all is not well one bite at a time. What if the traffic means the plague has infected this place, too? What if one of those who turned made their way up here and infected the monks of the Smiling Eye? I swallow down my worries. There's no point in borrowing trouble. Perhaps they will prove to be truly good and will not have turned.

I don't want to make you more nervous, but in my experience, people don't shut themselves away from the world because they are good. They do it because they are clever enough to realize that they are evil, and yet they still have enough compassion to try to shield the world from it.

Great. That makes these monks prime candidates to turn.

Might I suggest taking a more circuitous route to the monastery and getting a good look at it before you ride in where they can see you?

It's a good idea. And the last time he had a good idea I ignored it and disaster ensued. This time, I won't be so stupid.

That's very reasonable.

"I'm going to scout the area to be sure it's safe for Armend," I tell the duke as I dismount. "Keep out of sight. If the way is safe, I'll let you know. If I'm not back in an hour, then I'm in trouble and you should both run." The duke opens his mouth to protest and I roll my eyes. "Don't tell me you've decided to hunt monsters, too?"

He shakes his head "no" even as the priest makes a drowsy

holy sign with his hands. I offer the reins of my horse to the duke.

"Take care," he whispers and I nod.

As I slip into the woods, I hear a whisper behind me. The priest is asking Stekkan, "Is she safe?"

"None of us are safe," Stekkan murmurs.

He's not wrong. I slip further into the dense forest, clinging to my sword. I am not skilled in woodcraft.

You're telling me. You sound like a new recruit during training.

I huff my irritation. It's not my fault that I didn't expect this would be in my future. If I knew, I would have read fewer books and tried harder at sneaking around.

Something tells me that even pain of death wouldn't have been enough to keep you from reading books. His resonant voice burrs at that and I suppress a shiver. I could listen to his voice all day. It seems like every time he speaks it goes deeper and deeper into my heart, stripping me down by layers as it seeks the very core of who I am. He shifts his tone to instruction. *Keep your balance on the balls of your feet. Focus on knowing where your feet land rather than seeing far ahead. I'll keep a lookout for enemies. You look to be sure you don't trip, or slip, or crack a twig.*

I do as I am told and before long, I'm quieter. It feels like far too long before the thick trees before us begin to thin. My heart leaps at the sight of the white building between the scrubby growth. It's two stories tall with a slender bell tower on one end. Someone is coming out of it.

Relief floods through me. This is a normal place. We can leave Armend here, and maybe even stock up on supplies. There might even be food.

My stomach growls at the thought and my next step isn't quite as careful. A twig breaks. I'm not worried because I don't mind if the people at the cloister see me. The Smiling Eye and his cloister can't be too upset to see a friendly face, right?

Freeze.

I obey. And that's when I see them. There's a ring of guards just out from the treeline. They stand very still, and they watch in every direction. Colored smoke billows around each of them and the guard nearest to me has a small fissure running down his cheek. It glows a vibrant red like the smoke swirling around his head and shoulders. I have to bite my lip hard to keep from yelping.

Don't look directly at them. People can feel when you do that. And don't move.

They're the Princess's guards. That's her livery they're wearing.

She'll be here, too. You were right that they would take this road and right to guess they wouldn't be able to move much faster than we did. Little did you know, she thinks so closely to how you think that she went to the same place.

Now what?

Now, we need to get down on the ground. But we need to wait until we can move without being seen.

I shiver. I feel exposed here and I hate it. I wish I could see Vargaard. Just seeing him would ease this.

Shift your right foot very slightly forward.

I do, and to my surprise, it turns my body just enough to see my shadow. He's mostly invisible – just a dark blur instead of anything substantial, but I can see the faintest hint of a smile on that dark shadow face and looking through it, I feel like I can see just a tiny hint of who he was a thousand years ago before he committed unthinkable crimes and turned his soul over to be punished.

Was he a child? Did Nakuraki have children?

I don't know. I can't remember being a child. I have that one, terrible memory of a family and then nothing. And since I have been attached to this blade, I have seen no others of my kind. If they are out there, then they are few or far away.

I don't know what to say in the face of such loneliness.

Now, sink slowly down. That's right. Slowly.

I sink down into the brush until I'm sitting in the dried grasses and pine cones. They jab into me uncomfortably.

No one can see you here as long as you are silent, but you must wait until dark to return to the others. Are you sure that you want to?

They have my horse.

They are not much of a help to you. They merely slow you down.

He thought royalty from our neighboring country and a priest who had maps of every secret place in the land were slowing me down too much?

Well, I'll admit that they are also useful. Slow and useful. Like turtles.

I roll my eyes. At least I can do that silently. And carefully, very carefully, I pull my father's book from my pocket and begin to read it. That I can do silently, too.

Yes, but you can't watch for danger while you're reading.

That's what he is for.

I'm a quick reader. He might tease me for not being able to do much else. I might even regret it myself. I can't snare food for us – although I can tell you the names of five types of snares. I can't track my enemy and tell you how far up the road they are – although I can tell you how Siseri lost the battle of Ghenshi because his opponent left false tracks for him. I *can* read.

My eyes slip over the words fast as rain over an oiled cloak. And as I read, I absorb the meaning of the book and I grow colder and colder inside.

This book is old. It's so old that I shouldn't be carrying it around with me. It should be under glass somewhere or locked in a drawer – like where my father left it.

It's so ancient that the beginning is entirely written in ancient Tyrillic. It starts with a long poetic passage that I skim, but the idea of it is basically that men are evil and warrior men are doubly evil and that it's hard to really cut down evil when it comes calling.

And I already know that because it's been the nightmare I've been living for the past few days.

Then it dives into how very clever one great sage was and how he decided he could forge seven weapons to fight against evil – but they needed great power and he certainly wasn't going to pull it from beyond the veil like his enemies did – whatever that meant. There was a lot of flowery language and obfuscating, but in the end, I realized that they somehow subjugated seven prisoners and fed them to the blade. Nakuraki. But – and this was key – they had to actually be essentially good beings or the process didn't work. Nakuraki who felt guilty but weren't actually guilty.

And this is where I pause because the horror of this is enormous. It means that guilty as Vargaard feels, he is innocent or the binding that reduced him to a parasite soul living in something's shadow wouldn't have worked.

I don't know if I should tell him. My heart is racing at the thought that I should. It feels too enormous. It feels like too much. What will he do if I tell him?

That thought plagues me as I get through to the journal entries. There's a lot about the swords and how they were hidden and hints of their power. I wish I had more time to take it all in, but I'll have to do that later.

Something is moving.

I jam the book back in my pocket and grab the sword in both hands. I can barely make out words on the page. The sun is fully set and darkness swells over the forest.

Stand up slowly.

I stand and he is right there beside me in the long shadow formed by the lights they've lit in the cloister.

Listen. You need to make a decision. It feels like he's right there against me – because he is. He's not even a breath away and knowing that I can't see him in the night doesn't dull the feeling of intimacy that brings. *You can go back to the priest and the duke, but they might not be there anymore and even if they are, they can't stay here in this cloister. You'll have to send them on without you. And if I move you out of here, I might not be able to get you back in again.*

Why not?

Your woodcraft needs work.

My stupid cheeks grow hot, which is ridiculous. I know I'm bad at this.

If you snap a stick – and you will – then you'll alert them. If you do it more than once, they'll give chase. I'm pretty sure I can dispatch a handful of guards but then they'll all be watching. You can't just kill half of them and then dance back in and steal their gem.

So, what should I do?

We could go after it right now. In the twilight, when it's hardest to see and the guards are changing shifts, their bellies growling in hunger.

It sounds risky. And I'd promised the duke I'd go back. But it will be better to go back with the gem in hand. And I really believe that Vargaard can help me get it.

If I were to bare my heart to you, I would say that I prefer you abandon this quest completely. I do not like the risk involved. But if you are set on it, then this is the lesser risk – to act when they do not expect it.

I am not going back. There is no place to run *to* that won't be just like this soon if I don't stop it.

My stomach heaves, reminding me that just because my brain is denying the risk, doesn't mean my body is going along with it. I ignored my stomach and nod in the semi-darkness.

"We'll have to move fast," I tell my bodyguard.

Follow my directions exactly, and I promise to get you out alive.

These days, that is the best kind of promise anyone can give me.

I grit my teeth, clench the sword in both my hands, and nod. I am as ready as I'll ever be.

NAKURAKI

I should tell her about the second dawn so it doesn't take her by surprise.

I should have told her before, but I thought she understood and I didn't realize that she had no idea at all how the sword and the shadow work until I vanished into the sword to heal. And now she is so happy that I'm back again and I didn't expect that.

I'm overwhelmed by her warmth toward me. It's like seeing the face of beauty for the first time. It snatches away my breath and my thoughts all at once. I could watch her forever. I could memorize every movement and catch my breath with every sigh.

It's like a forest fire in my soul – consuming all my uncertainties and doubts, searing me with its sheer intensity. I do not want to sow doubt again. I want only to live in the firm certainty that my life begins and ends with her.

And one dawn is already past. Only one more remains until it is complete.

Besides, she is fighting her heart battle now. She is taking the risk she must to set things right. I can't interrupt that. Not even with something this important.

Every scrap of my mind and soul must go into her protection

now. I can spare nothing for hopes or dreams beyond that –
nothing for the inevitable fear that seizes me at making myself
mortal.

I've waited for a thousand years for something I didn't know
I was waiting for and now that I've found it, I refuse to lose my
chance because I hesitated. I won't hesitate. I will leap with both
feet, and if the darkness takes me, then it will not have taken a
coward.

Chapter Nineteen

We pass through the ring of guards and up to the back steps of the cloister in a whirl of Vargaard's curt instructions and my quick obedience. I don't even know how he finds the blind spots he sends me through. One moment a guard is looking, the next, as he looks away, Vargaard orders me to move. My bodyguard sees in all directions, anticipates every idle movement of the bored guards. He judges my capabilities perfectly.

My heart is in my throat waiting for a face to turn toward me or an ear to pick up on my movements, but it doesn't happen. And even with my breath caught in my chest, I know that it is all because of Vargaard and his smooth skill. He is born of shadow and he slips me through their ring of security as if I am a shadow, too.

If we are going to keep going on these adventures, I will have to learn my own stealth and speed. My whole task in this is to be fast and to keep from being seen.

I cling to the sword like it is my lifeline on a ship in a storm. It's growing heavier all the time in my tired arms, but if I sheathe it, my injuries and exhaustion weigh me down more than the sword ever could. It has the added effect of reminding me that Vargaard is real – that this isn't all some crazy dream of mine. That's a reminder I need right now as I slip into the backdoor of a cloister with only my shadow for safety.

The cloister is built like a long narrow house but with many doors around the outside. I haven't been here before and I don't know my way. Vargaard nudges me toward the central door at the very back and it's in there that I go. People are coming and going into all the other doors and my heart is in my throat. I fully expect someone to be just inside this large door.

The little doors on a building like this are likely cells for their monks. It's the only reason to have so many doors – so that they can come and go easily without disturbing one another. They won't access the main room of the building. That will only be accessed from the doors at the front and back of the building.

Then why have one building at all? Why not have many small ones?

Saves on the price to build it perhaps. Or perhaps it is based on a tenant of their faith. I don't know the Smiling Eye god so I cannot say for sure. Here, ease the door gently closed behind you. Slip one step to the left.

And that's when I realize why no one is using this door.

Don't scream!

It's a close call. I nearly scream. I still want to even though I don't. The scream is like a cat in my throat trying to claw its way out. I swallow it down and it makes me ill.

There are bodies piled here – a dozen at least. They've been thrown into a heap in the middle of the floor of what was once a kitchen, their white cassocks stained a terrible crimson. I make out an eye embroidered on the front of one cassock – open and unblinking just like the eyes of the monk wearing it.

I don't look further than that. I don't want to see. What I don't look at can't crawl down my throat with my scream and haunt me forever.

Good. They won't come here. That makes this a safe entry.

Good? That was not my reaction to this!

Easy now, Star of my Morning. Easy. Battle is a place for practicality and not poetry. There's no poetry in butchering a man like a pig.

I want to be ill.

Then do it quickly and soundlessly.

I get myself under control, clinging to the wall. I hate how casual he is in his order.

I'm here to protect your back, not coddle you. We can still flee. We don't have to do this. I can get you out that door and to the treeline before you know it.

No. I am resolved to get that gem and end this.

In that case, pull yourself together and slip around the bodies. There are two exits into the main building. One is the stairs leading up and one goes to the main gallery. Which will it be?

If there's a gallery, maybe there will be a balcony. I need to see better. I take the stairs.

Slowly now. Stairs creak.

I ease my way up.

When I get to the top, I am rewarded. It is a balcony. There's a small wall about waist high all the way around it and benches set in front of the wall so that you could sit there unseen but listening to what goes on below.

For prayers. Look up.

I look up to the peak of the roof. Someone has taken great pains to hang a carved wooden eye the size of a dinner table from the roof with chains. It turns very slightly, and I shiver. Whoever carved the eye made it look very real. It seems to be looking right at me.

We won't be able to see over the wall unless you get right up to it, but someone could be hiding at the other side of the balcony and you wouldn't know. That low wall would disguise them.

I pause, listening. I should check to see if there is someone on the other side of the balcony. I should investigate the whole place to be sure. But as I stand here listening, words drift up from below and I freeze in place so I can listen.

"Five days isn't long, Whitehaus. Are you certain it will be enough time to sway the remaining priesthoods?" The voice is gruff and earnest.

I creep forward until I'm right up against the low wall, straining to hear every word. This is important.

"We've been over this and over this, General." General? I feel as though a cold wind has blown up around me. "The army. The priesthood. The magistrates. We have the people in place to take them. All we need is the right event to set everything in motion. You can't just seize power or people revolt. You need a pretext, and this illness will be the perfect pretext. The people will be afraid. They will look to the officials and the priests for guidance and we will give it to them."

"It will need to be fast," the General's voice is low enough that I have to strain to hear it. "Other cities will hear about it and keep visitors out. If they do, your plan will fail. The illness will not spread, and the king will be able to rally sympathetic nobles to his cause. Not everyone will want to bow to Princess Jendaya. She is untried. So you'll need to get the priests turned quickly." He sounds nervous at the end like he thinks the princess might be listening and might not approve. Where is the princess? I would have expected her to be down in that council.

"Must we have the same discussions over and over? You're like a dog with a bone, Ferdown. You chew and chew at the same thing hoping the taste will change."

General Ferdown. I know that name. I swallow nervously. Jendaya has powerful allies.

"I'm just cautious. Coups are risky things. You must time them right or the people leading them die quickly – whether from loyalists or the graspers at their backs."

"And how is that any different from any other time? We are all subject to the whims of the times and the masses. That's why the princess's plan is ingenious. With this, we can double our power with half the trouble and finally build what Cragspear should always have been – an empire."

Mercy save me from men and their empires.

But there's nothing here we didn't know before – except maybe that General Ferdown and Lord Whitehaus are a part of this. We still need the gem. We still don't know where it is. I ease myself up on shaky legs to look out over the small wall.

There are maybe a dozen of them around a table with unmatched chairs surrounding it and maps scattered between the remains of dinner. I can only see the tops of their heads.

It's a war room – or as much of one as can be achieved with just one wall and a few paces between it and a heap of bodies. Or maybe all war rooms are laid out beside the first victims. How would I know?

I don't see a glowing green gem.

And I don't see the princess, which makes the back of my neck prickle.

What I *do* see makes my stomach turn. Every one of the people around the table below is wreathed in writhing smoke. It twists around them like it's trying to strangle them in cords of midnight blue or strands of emerald or jagged lines of charcoal. Some of the people reach up to stroke or pet the creatures manifesting themselves in the smoke and one of them has a fissure running down his face just like the one that ran down the face of that poor man in the pink smoke.

From what I can tell, once the avatar crosses over there are two choices – either the corricle masters it and is like your friend Jendaya with new strength and powers brought from the world beyond, or the avatar masters the corricle like your poor husk of a mayor and the human part rips and shrivels and the avatar deforms it.

And then what?

Who can say? I doubt they'll survive long in a broken husk.

I shiver. I feel ill watching them in their fine clothes with their grand plans and their lives ebbing away.

"Here for the gem?"

I'm so startled by the quiet words that I stumble backward. I feel Vargaard hiss as I hurry to get the point of my sword up. His hiss is a dragon awakened to an intruder. It sizzles down every nerve under my skin.

To my horror, Jendaya is on the balcony across from me, watching me with glittering eyes. She reaches out and strokes the nose of her azure smoke unicorn as it appears in the air beside her, but her face is unmarred by cracks, and her eyes are not glazed with pain. She's fully in command of herself and she leans forward like a snake, her eyes glittering with excitement.

Vargaard is right. There are two paths, and hers is the powerful one.

"I wondered if you would come back for it," she says and she seems smug – like a girl who knows she's wearing the most expensive dress at a dance. "I know *I* wouldn't forget it once I saw it. He waited until my eighteenth birthday to show it to me – which was smarter than I'd usually give him credit for. That was just a month ago. Did you know that?"

I back up another step, shaking my head as she starts to work her way around the balcony as if she thinks I'm the mouse to her snake.

"I couldn't stop thinking about it. I couldn't stop wondering what I would do someday when it was in my possession. I wouldn't keep it hidden like that old fool did. But I don't have to be my father, do I? I could take it now and use it now. And I did."

"Why are you telling me this?" I ask her. Beneath us, voices rise in an argument. Her counselors and generals don't even know I am here.

Lure her in. Stop backing up. I can take her.

"He said he'd have me married off by the end of the season. I'm an asset, you know, not a person. Can you believe that? Do you know what it's like to be told you're going to be married off to someone you didn't choose?"

"Yes," I say. It's hard to stay still like Vargaard has asked. Every instinct wants me to run.

"Well. Then I guess you know." She snaps her fingers dramatically and then waves them. "But it's gone, and you're too late."

I go cold as she edges around the corner of the balcony and starts to speed up.

A little closer. Just don't back up.

My shadow is so close to me that I'll have to let her get very close. There's no tail at all in front of me. She'll have to be close enough to touch me.

She seems to want the same thing. Her unicorn flickers in and out of existence. She's just steps away.

Come on!

"What's gone?" I ask. And my heart drops to somewhere around the bottom of my belly because I already know what she's going to say. She's going to tell me that this final risk was for nothing.

She's almost in reach of me when she confirms my fear.

"The gem," she says with a savage grin. "I sent it away."

Just one more step. Bring her in closer!

But I can hardly think.

"Why are you telling me this," I say again. But my heart is racing, fear spiking through my veins hot and angry. I shouldn't have taken the risk. It's been for nothing. Nothing!

She takes the final step and Vargaard lunges, turning corporeal just before his hand reaches out and catches her throat in its grasp. He's wearing a ring on his index finger, I note, and his cuff is of fine wool with lace spilling out from under it. He catches her slender throat in his hand and his beautiful face twists into something ugly.

Got her!

I feel a rush of relief. Her unicorn disappears in a puff of aqua smoke as her eyes go wide with fear.

A floorboard squeaks behind me.

And before I can turn, something crashes on my head and pain fills my mind.

I slip into blackness.

CHAPTER TWENTY

I blink awake. Pain shoots through my head and my thoughts are slow. I try to move but my head is caught in something – no, it's my hair. It's being held in place. Any move rips at it. I hiss. Princess Jendaya fills my vision, clutching her throat, muttering curses in a hoarse voice. She sees I'm looking at her and her eyes go hard. Her sudden blow takes me by surprise.

Heavy rings rip my skin as light flares across my vision. I think I cry out but I don't know. Everything is pain right now. I blink away waves of darkness, trying to scramble against the hands holding me. Something hot pours from my nose. Blood. I puff out a breath to try to clear it. I've only been unconscious for a moment. That much I can tell. I need to think.

My thoughts are too thick to form. My breathing hitches.

Someone lights a torch behind me and like a black dragon leaping, Vargaard springs to life.

He shakes himself, looking around us, assessing. His eyes narrow.

He needs to wait. Jendaya's about to say something.

"I knew you'd come and give me this," the princess says, snatching the sword from the ground. My sword. That's what

I need. She seems triumphant. "It was in the book your father kept. The Seven Swords. All of them need to be together to conquer what the green gem brings. But you already know that. It's why you took the book and the sword and nothing else. You know you need them to stop me. It's your plan. But you're too late. The gem is already on its way to the capital."

I'd taken those things because they were mine. How did she leap to the conclusion that it was about the gem? They wouldn't be enough anyway. Not with the gem already on its way to the capital. Not unless I can stop it before it gets there. And I can't. I'm surrounded. My only ally will be overwhelmed. Just like he was when he protected Valiant.

No. His voice is a rumbling hum of fury.

It will be okay. I can accept the end. And he will go back to the sword's shadow and protect another.

Not this time. This time it's —

Jendaya grabs my chin between her fingers, her smile triumphant.

"And now I have it all. The sword, and your life."

I'm an idiot. I don't see her second blow coming until it impacts on my injured nose.

Vargaard's snarl rips through my brain. His fury bursts past whatever he was trying to tell me. I can't hold him back.

She touched you! She hurt you.

He dives in a rush of shadow and lifts the princess, tossing her to the side. I hear a shriek as she flies through the air, the sword clattering to the ground.

Whatever has me by the hair drops me. All I feel is pain in my ringing head, aching scalp, and my battered nose. It's broken. I'm sure of it.

Roll.

I roll and land on the sword. My hands close around the hilt and I scramble to my feet, sword held high. I'm gasping with relief as it takes my pain. I'm lightheaded, but I can function. I can move. I spin in time to bring up the point as someone charges right into me.

Our eyes meet, and I realize in horror that my attacker has run himself onto the blade of my sword when the pommel hits my belly, knocking the wind out of me. His momentum pushes us both back into the low wall of the balcony. I stumble, pulling the sword free with difficulty. It's jammed between his ribs. He's gargling on blood and I can't get it out. I wrench it side to side and yank. It comes free of the bone and I fall back as my enemy slumps to the floor. I don't even see his face. I just see horror.

My arms ache from his weight twisting them around and I still can't suck in a full breath but I steady myself on my feet and look up. I must be stronger. I must be faster.

My shadow trails toward the stairway door. The torch is out, fallen somewhere. The only light comes from the opening of the main room, reflecting off the polished wood eye emblem. It's not enough to throw much of a shadow and Vargaard is pulled backward with me. He battles the creature that held me a moment ago – a cracked husk with a billowy smoke creature pouring up from his head and neck. It gives the illusion of two sets of arms – though one pair is his billowy grey arms and the other is the human arms hanging lifelessly at his sides.

Vargaard ducks and spins but he can't reach. My shadow is too short.

I stumble forward, still trying to take a breath. The air is caught somewhere and I can't pull it in.

More.

I force myself to take another step toward the monstrosity. My head is spinning. I see little stars float across my vision like angry comets. Another. It's only on the third step that I realize the door to the stairway is clogged with more fighters trying to get around the first one and at us.

She called them. When you thought she was snapping her fingers to make a point, it was a signal. Listen. The argument below has ceased.

But maybe that was from when they heard all the fighting up here. I finally suck in a ragged breath and my head clears.

From the corner of my eye, I see Princess Jendaya picking herself up. Her face is already starting to swell from her fall and fury lights her eyes.

"Grab her." Her voice holds enough authority to launch ships. "She has what we want. Kill her if you must."

There's no way out but through. But I don't like this through.

Jendaya is moving cautiously toward me. No matter what anyone says to me about her, I'll never doubt her courage or cleverness. She's shown both. And she's squinting at me like she knows Vargaard is there somewhere and that she just can't see him. She's not as easily fooled as the duke.

Somehow, she knows.

"I knew that sword granted some kind of power," she says,

consideringly.

The husk with the avatar spilling out of it lunges toward me, swiping at me with his huge smoke paw.

Vargaard flings himself at me and throws me out of the way. It's the first time I actually feel his body. And I remember what he said. I'd only ever feel him in moments of violence. I'm surprised by how he feels – warm and hard with muscle. His breath gusts across my face and the softness of his hair touches my cheek as he takes the blow meant for me and then rolls off me and back to standing in my shadow. My eyes are wide and I'm frozen for a half a second. I'm feeling too many things at once.

I'm feeling terror as the husk shuffles further into the room and the men in the stairway flood into the balcony, fanning out to surround me.

I'm feeling anxiety as Jendaya stalks toward me, her eyes fixed on the sword that I've brought up in front of me again. And I'm feeling physical attraction like I've never felt before at the mere brush with Vargaard. I want to feel his hand in mine. I want to reach out and touch that silky soft hair.

It's madness. I'm about to be killed. My quest was for nothing. I should be thinking about that.

Maybe it's because I'm about to die. My mind wants to feel everything. It doesn't want to leave a single thing unexperienced when there's only so much left to grasp. I let it feel everything. What can it hurt?

Vargaard glances back and my eye meets his for a moment and my heart leaps. All I see is those bright eyes and that look of possessive worry.

What's wrong? Are you hurt? You aren't moving.

He has to turn back to fight and I swallow at the sight of his shadow muscles straining to push back the bigger foe. I shake my head and hold my blade higher.

Sheathe it and get up on the wall.

Is he joking?

When I joke you'll know it. I'm very funny. Wall. Now.

I sheathe the sword awkwardly and scramble up the low wall, but my movement shrinks my shadow and suddenly Vagaard's right there, panting from exertion, smelling of sweat and black pepper. And he's a shadow. He shouldn't smell of anything. He shouldn't make me want to lean into his heat and suck in deep breaths.

Now, you jump.

What?

His shadow eyes look deep into mine as a battle cry roars from those surrounding us. They're about to charge.

Trust me. Jump.

I can't make myself do it. The fall is the height of four men. I'll die. Or break something more than my nose.

His expression goes grim and then suddenly he's completely corporeal. I gasp. His hand shoots out and hits me right in the middle of the chest.

I'm tumbling backward before I can process what has happened. The wall is getting smaller. The surprised faces looking down from it are smaller, too. I open my mouth to scream and a shadow is sucked over the edge with me. He clings to me, wraps himself around me until all I smell is darkness and ground black pepper and I cling to him mentally with every thought, every hope.

It's not the worst way to die.

We hit the ground and the breath goes out of me again. My head hurts like it's been split down the middle for an avatar to come out. I feel it to make sure it isn't split apart.

But he's broken my fall somehow. He's wheezing in my long shadow, clutching his chest.

"Vargaard," I gasp.

He looks up, flashes me a confident grin – what? – and charges past me in my long shadow, disarming the general in the pretty waistcoat before the man can get his sword tip up.

Vargaard doesn't stop and I stumble after him, snatching a candle from the table and lifting it high to give him as much shadow as I dare.

I keep the candle high and keep a steady pace forward, ignoring the shouts from the balcony above. I don't dare pause or it will hold Vargaard up. He's already at the end of my shadow, battling a monster boiling up out of what was once a man. It lunges for him, pale yellow smoke billowing around it like a fire made of wet spruce. Out of the curling smoke comes a head like a barking dog and as I watch, the man's face splits apart.

The man – Whitehaus I think, when I hear his voice – screams as the dog rips him down the middle and spills out of him. As soon as it is free, it seems to expand and then contract again and unlike the others I've seen, it sheds its human shell completely and lunges for us.

The room clears as chairs scrape and shouts ring out. I didn't even realize there were still people here. I've been to caught up in this single moment, this battle. But now, even the dog's allies are fleeing the room.

Vargaard charges, laying into the dog with his dark shadow blade. Ribbons of smoke are carved off and disappear into the air of the cloister.

I hurry behind Vargaard, dancing forward with his advances and backward with his retreats, watching his every movement for cues on how to move and what to do.

He's lightning fast. I can't keep up. But if I'm conscious and careful I can keep from hindering him by keeping his shadow where it needs to be so he can bend and stretch and fight.

He's a blur of darkness and power fighting against the smoke and roars of the monster. Darting. Weaving. Slashing. And then, suddenly, his battle is over and the smoke is dissipating while screams happen somewhere in the balcony and stairway.

Vargaard turns to me, chest heaving, still corporeal for this moment as the violence fades. He reaches for my face as if he means to cup it and my breath hitches in my throat.

There's something in his dark shadow eyes – something deep and powerful. Something that rings with pain and desire all rolled up into one. And I don't care about the feet thundering down the stairs. I don't care about the shouts and the sound of Jendaya's voice snapping over the rest as she brings them to order. All I want is that touch on my face from this – my guardian, my protector.

But the bare second it takes to reach for me dissipates him and his hand passes through my cheek. My disappointment is echoed in his eyes.

I understand your fight, Ilsaletta. His words are a caress. *I have fought hopeless battles, too. Now, come, we must flee while we can.*

There's no one in the gallery – yet. Their sounds are all around us.

I see a leather satchel to one side sewn with crystal beads. I snatch it up. It is likely Jendaya's and anything of hers might have things I need in it.

We dive through the door at the back of the room – the door that none of our enemies went through – and enter the room full of corpses. I shut the door carefully as the first yells enter the gallery behind us.

Another shout echoes outside the door of the small room.

We're surrounded.

I open my mouth to scream and Vargaard puts a finger over his lips.

The bodies. Put out the candle and hide under them. Our enemies will pass by.

My gaze snags on the corpses. The sounds outside the room are getting louder. They're almost upon us and yet I can't. I just can't.

You can. You must.

I can't.

He wraps his shadow around me like a hug – like the kind of hug that presses whole bodies together.

I gasp.

I will shelter you. But now, tie your line of courage to the rock and do what you must. We will not fail and die here.

I bite my lip, try to think about anything else that I can and then with great care, I approach the back of the pile of bodies and find a small dip to huddle in. I shove the bag in first and then I crouch down over it.

Ilsaletta, I know you are trying. But merely crouching here will not be enough. There are too many of them for me in the gallery and too many outside this door. We need the element of surprise. And that means you need to hide.

I shudder.

Close your eyes. Put your arms over your head. I'll do this.

But he could only be corporeal if he were violent.

I will be violent.

I do as he says, and I try not to flinch when a dead weight – a *literal dead* weight – slams beside me. I bite my lip and I don't scream. But I want to. It smells of death. And it used to be a person.

It's sacrilege. It's wrong.

But the way Vargaard has attacked this body has left its cassock hanging over me, disguising me from notice. Which is not enough to keep me from gagging underneath it.

I am guilty of desecrating the dead. I am guilty of treating them as things and not people. I am no better than those who killed them.

That's where you're wrong. You are better, Ilsaletta. You're better than your land deserves.

Death fills my nose and my mouth until I want to spew out everything I've ever eaten. It fills me up with unshed tears and revulsion rolls through me like a fever. In my shadow, I feel Vargaard close. He can't touch me. He can't help with this. And yet I feel as if his arms are around me and he croons gentle words into my mind.

Just like me. You're just like me. You never wanted this. You're only surviving it and trying not to let your soul dip so deep into the river of blood that the stains never come out.

But he said his stains never would come out.

Maybe I was wrong. Maybe we're all wrong. Life and death – what are they? I can claim neither for myself anymore. We are feathers in the wind, but we are also heavy of heart and burdened of soul. What we are, who we are – can we really know before the story is over?

I don't have an answer to that. I want to curl up in a ball and sob until I die. But if I do that, then Jendaya will leave here and become Queen and kill half the world and who will stop her when the whole of Cragspear backs her? The only time to stop her is now. The only place is here.

And I will hold onto you, Ilsaletta. I won't let you face it alone. I will walk with you and though I may not touch you, my arms will shield you, and though I cannot carry you, I will carry your burdens. Though I cannot feed you, I will not let you go hungry. Sick or well, dying or vibrant, destitute or rich, beautiful or withered, innocent or drenched in blood – I will cling to you and guard you, I will honor you and lift you up.

There are wedding vows less full.

Indeed.

And yet he's sworn this in the past again and again.

I will confess something to you. I –

He breaks off.

Someone is pushing at the bodies, searching.

"She won't be in there, Raggern. No one would hide in a pile of bodies," someone calls from the door.

I try not to shiver at his words. The searching stops and voices call from too far to be heard. The sound of them is intent. They are searching for me.

Patience. We bide our time until the opportunity is right.

What does he want to confess? Anything to take my mind off what I am doing.

There are many vows a Nakamuri can make. The vow I made you, I have never made before. The vow I make now is also fresh. Never before have I made promises this deep. Never before have I put my own soul to rest in the heart of another.

Then why me? Does he have a weakness for young girls? I grit my teeth. I don't like that idea at all.

You wound me, Ilsaletta. That's not it at all. It's ... something too all encompassing to explain.

He is going to need to try.

You ... are a bright star. The dawn of the sun at day. The glory of the light.

Those are pretty things to say but they don't mean anything that makes sense to me.

I sense him fumbling, looking for how to say what he means. His voice drops even lower than normal and there is a hint of pain as his words sink beneath my skin.

In that closet – desperate and afraid – you made me think of my sister all those years ago. But it's more than that. You don't just make me think of Asgaard. You make me think of myself when I was a young warrior. You aren't as weak as you fear you are. We are the same in some ways. And yet, you're so much more. You're … you are light. With you, my life dawns fresh.

I still don't really understand.

I need you to trust me, too. We can be a powerful force together. Trust that I am yours, soul and shadow.

I bite my lip. I don't want to trust completely. It feels like too much, too soon. I trusted all the people in my home and village. I trusted my father would always be there for me. Look what trust has brought me?

It's brought you me.

Trust, it seems, is just another place where I will have to be brave.

It's time to move. Are you ready?

I want to take a deep breath, but I know better than to do that. Instead, I push and shove my way out, gasping when my face is finally free. I know I'm crying. I'll lash out at anyone who mentions it. I should be crying. All these poor people in this pile were sons and brothers at one time. And yeah, they were weird men who lived in the woods and worshiped a wooden eye. But they didn't deserve to be made not-men just because Jendaya wanted to sleep in their beds without the trouble of them hanging around complaining.

Look in her bag.

I search it quickly. There's nothing here but a spare dress, some powders and lotions, and a tiny hand mirror. One look at my face in the mirror makes me draw back. I'm streaked in blood.

Bring it with you. When this is done, you'll want to wear something that is not covered in death.

I hurry to obey, pulling the strap of the satchel across my body. She's taken so much from me that it hardly feels like enough to steal her spare dress. I need to steal all her terrible plans, too.

My thoughts make me brave. I stumble to the door.

Sword out, Vargaard reminds me. *This is the tricky part. We need to move fast but not draw attention to ourselves. We need to get to the treeline and the river.*

Why the river?

Speed. These monks may have left a boat. The river was swollen when we saw it from the old road. If we find a boat, we can leave here quickly and soundlessly.

And the duke and the priest?

They wait at the bridge. The river will pass the bridge. We can stop there if you wish.

It's a solid plan. I'm ready.

I open the door and slip into the night.

Chapter Twenty-One

He leads me through the night, one step at a time – an expert guiding the hand of a novice piece by piece. Around us, the camp surrounding the cloister is in chaos. It is easy to slip between the long shadows surrounding the large building and into the night.

Most of the activity seems to be taking place around the front door. With the attention of our adversaries there, we sneak into the treeline. It's not until my foot breaks a twig and nothing happens that I feel like I can take a breath. We're out of the heart of their lair and slipping along the edge of the trees toward the rush of the river.

We've been hiding for about twenty minutes. It takes even longer to creep along the edges of the camp. The river is within paces when we spot a bump in the darkness.

A boat. Vargaard sounds triumphant and my heart soars with him. He's right. It's here like he'd thought, and we can flee in that on the swollen river.

My hands settle on the weatherworn wood and all I feel is relief as I right the boat and drop Jendaya's bag into it. There are a pair of paddles under it. I throw them hastily into the hull.

I'm about to shove it toward the swell of the Bubblethroat when a voice pierces the night.

I freeze. Over the babble of the river, I barely hear the shouts – but they're there. I have to concentrate to make out the words.

"I know you are out there, Ilsaletta Redtide. You flee in vain. I have your two lap dogs here with me."

It's Princess Jendaya.

At any other time of my life, if I had thought of a princess I would have thought of parties and lace and pretty dresses. I wouldn't have thought of this relentless, determined, powerful woman. She's only my age and she dwarfs me in resolution.

Don't sell yourself short.

And powerful generals and counsellors follow her.

Carrion birds follow anyone who will lead them to carcasses.

And she has set a trap for me. While I was hiding and thinking I was outsmarting her, escaping her, avoiding her – she was hard at work. She'd found the duke and the priest and now she was waiting for me to come for them.

Then don't go for them.

He'd promised to help me if I trusted him.

And I will, but you can't bring down the princess if you're captured and I am only one shadow. I can't kill all her allies at once. If I try, I will fail, and you will die.

My hand runs along the worn wood. It would be so easy to slip down the river like he wants.

And then you can return to deal with Jendaya at a time you pick. In a place you choose.

The rumble of his voice is so sincere. It resonates deep under my skin and through all my protests to my very core.

And he is right in front of me. The full moon lights the area so brightly that my shadow pools at my feet. He stands in it, and the silver limning of moonlight almost makes him look fully corporeal. Otherworldly beauty lights his face – frozen in time to make him look barely older than my nineteen years. At most, he looks twenty-three or twenty-four rather than a millenia old. And the look of angst and misery on his face isn't helping him look any older. I didn't know ancient creatures pouted.

Old I may be, but I was only reborn yesterday, and you'd be mistaken to think I've matured. I'm frozen – frozen in the state I was in when I was taken. Frozen in this body. I do not age. I do not shift. I do not grow stale or sweaty.

His dark-lined eyes flash in the moonlight.

I thought I could not change.

Is that not true?

His hand lifts to nearly cup my face and he leans in so close that if he was human I'd feel his breath on my lips.

Don't risk yourself for the pretty duke. Be reasonable. Please. You carry my soul in your shadow.

And yet, I asked the duke to wait for me. He was counting on me. It would be wrong to let him down.

It's wiser to wait. To assess. To find their weakness. We don't have to abandon him. But why not be careful with what is most precious to me. His tone is wheedling. *You are most precious to me. There's no need to risk yourself.*

"Come out, Ilsaletta." The princess's voice is faint. "I know you can hear me. I am instructing my men to start beating Duke Stekkan. They will continue until you arrive. And then you will exchange that sword and book for him. Fail to arrive in five minutes, and we will take a finger from him. Fail again, and we will take more. By morning, there will be no duke left at all."

That settles it. I must go after him.

Vargaard's face twists and he leans in so that there isn't even a breath between us.

Please he pleads against my lips. *I beg you, wait.*

It's like a kiss and a plea all at once. I breathe it in. There's no warmth, and yet it melts something inside me to the point of near bursting. There's no touch, and yet it seems to touch every part of me. I want to fall apart at the depth of that voice.

I will lose you if you go. I cannot keep them all away. And if I lose you, that will be the end. Please don't go, Ilsaletta. I have pledged you everything.

A pang of guilt goes through me. Because he has given me everything he has to give and yet I'm going to force him to fight for me against his will. I'm going to go back for Stekkan. And I'll likely die doing it.

Spare us that. Stay with me.

I step back and he gasps, his lips trembling in the moonlight. I wish with all my heart that I could touch him – that I could kiss him goodbye. But I can't. And I can't grant his wish, either.

I won't save myself at the expense of someone else.

You can't save them. Now he just sounds irritated. The burr in his voice is more pronounced. *It will just mean that all of us die together. If you get in the boat and go to sea, we'll find your father and we'll work together to reach him and to stop the princess.*

It's such an appealing offer and it's made with the most delicious, silky, warm voice in my mind. Every part of me wants to relent.

All but one. That one part of me where duty is housed raises its walls and screams. It doesn't matter what I want. It matters what I must. And I must not betray someone who trusted me.

"I can't," I gasp.

He shudders.

"I have to go back for him."

For him, he repeats and there's a mocking to his tone. I could have said "them," couldn't I? I should have. Because now he thinks I'm going back just for golden-jacket Stekkan.

His shadow form lifts a single eyebrow.

I had to try. I couldn't let us both die without trying first.

In the distance, there's a cry of pain. And another.

He can't even shut up for long enough to let you decide.

He's being beaten!

My heart is torn in two like wet bread. I take a stumbling step toward the cries and turn back. Only Vargaard isn't behind me. He's anchored to my shadow, so he's right here alongside me. His smirk turns bitter.

All light in this life is lost to me, he says grimly. *Even when I weave my soul into a wreath and lay it at your feet it is not enough to sway you.*

It's not like that.

Another cry – this time more of a scream of pain. I pick up my pace.

One of us is master and one is servant. He sounds so bitter that I flinch. *I have forgotten myself. Speak master, and I will obey.*

It's not like that. It's about saving a life. Doesn't he care about that?

His back is turned and though it is perfectly shaped and beautiful under his doublet, he has turned his back on me and that stabs me to the core.

His words are so quiet that I barely hear them over the screams. *The only life I care about saving is yours.*

There's no reasoning with him. And no changing my mind. I clench my jaw on an overwhelming emotion and the tears that threaten to spill from my eyes. I lift the blade of my sword. And I hurry toward the sounds.

I don't know if it's fury or despair or disappointment raging through me like a typhoon and I don't care. Vargaard made me feel this way about doing the right thing. I shouldn't have to be made to feel so awful about helping someone else. I feel like a fool for trusting him. I feel like a fool for thinking he was safe to listen to.

All I've done is try to protect you. Stop being so dramatic about it.

I will when he does.

But he won't. He's the king of drama.

I'm the king of nothing and the slave of everything and you are the one who holds my whip.

And that *isn't* dramatic? He is lying to himself.

One last try – please see sense and don't do this.

It's the "see sense" part that makes me run twice as fast. As if I am not being sensible. As if I'm the one who is a fool because I believe in being faithful. I hate that he is saying these things to me. And I hate that he might be right.

I run harder.

Chapter Twenty-Two

No one can fault Princess Jendaya's sense for the dramatic.
If anyone can top Vargaard it's her. She's had a bonfire built in
front of the monastery front steps. It dances and leaps – a demon
conjured for terror and harrowing. I'm nervous about what it
does to the shadows. None of them are steady, though they are
long and full. Vargaard will have room to maneuver – if he's still
going to fight with me.

*I am yours to the end. Angry or not. Despairing or not. I am your
blade and your protector.*

I don't have time to be grateful. I don't have time to think of
how unfair this is to him.

What was that? Unfair? Unreasonable?

I ignore him.

The fire illuminates the yard around the cloister and the nobles
and generals who are with Jendaya fan out to either side of where
she stands on the steps. Whitehaus is missing. With good reason.

Two of Jendaya's Silver Guard hold the duke between them.

His canary jacket is torn to shreds and hangs around him in rags. His face is bloodied and swelling. A third guard slugs him in the belly and he moans, spitting blood.

The rest of her guards ring the fire, their magic hosts swirling around them or bubbling out of them in whatever grotesque way they can. The one closest to me is so bent and twisted that I can't tell if he's human anymore. But others – like Jendaya's maid – look perfectly normal. In this darkness, their colored smoke is invisible, and their manifestations hidden. Does the maid have family in the capital? What does she think will happen to them when she returns with her ghastly mistress?

Eventually, I will need to puzzle out what all of this means. I'll need to think about whether they will all be overtaken and discarded like the mayor – Vlorence Wavemaker – or whether some can remain hidden and human-looking like Jendaya. I'll have to try to determine if she's still Jendaya or so possessed by a soul from beyond the veil that her human soul is overridden.

But now is not the time for that.

Now, I must be brave and swim into the shark's cave.

Jendaya sees me first. She knew I would come. Her smile has no innocence left in it.

"Ilsaletta," she says in her silken voice. "You've come to make a trade. Our little priest was just telling me how useful you can be."

I freeze for a moment.

Beside her in the shadow.

He's right. Armend crouches just behind her, his maps clutched in his hands and a look of fear across his face. But that can't be right. He didn't turn. That means he's good. And if he's good, how could he betray us?

Good people don't always agree on the right course. Just because he is good doesn't mean he's on your side.

But it should mean he isn't on *her* side. She's clearly wicked.

There's none so blind as those who will not see.

And he has those maps. I should have hidden them somewhere. I should have made sure they couldn't reach her. With those, she has hidden roads to drive her people secretly into the hearts of our neighboring nations.

Beside the princess, one of her advisors snickers and I feel my face go hot.

They're laughing at me. The girl who was betrayed by a priest. The girl who looks surprised by it. I want to look around the circle at all these people – if they're still people – and see who is laughing and who is bored and who is just plain evil. But it's surprisingly hard to keep track of everyone in a large group when there's just one of you to look. It's not like in the history books I read where it's all laid out so precisely. I feel like I should know about the failing trade of one of the nobles that drove him to align with the evil princess or maybe how the general nurses a grudge against the king that makes his daughter look like a better prospect to sit on the throne. Or maybe he's in debt and this is the only way to free himself. If this was a book, I would know all that.

But it isn't a book and going on adventures is so much more immediate and confusing than a book is. There are too many things to be watching for – too many things to try to keep track of.

My gaze keeps drifting back to the duke. His eyes are locked on me in a wordless plea. Still, after all this, the man sees me as his saviour.

And maybe you like that.

I push Vargaard's thoughts away. I'm already choked with all the things to pay attention to. I can't be distracted by his accusations, too.

"You offered a trade," I say in my calmest tone. I'm proud that my voice doesn't shake. They can't see that my knees are weak or that my mouth is dry. I certainly won't show them that, either. "The sword for the duke. Can I assume you're keeping the priest?"

She laughs and I know I'm in trouble. She plans to keep everything, including me.

You knew this was a trap. You're here now. Don't lose your nerve. Keep your back to the woods. We need a clear path of escape. You wouldn't really give up the sword, would you?

I'm not that much of a fool. I know how important this sword is. I learned my lesson last time. I need Vargaard. Without him, I have no way to fight at all.

"I think I will keep the clever Armend," Jendaya says, putting her hand on the priest's shoulder and drawing him into the light. I flex my fingers over the hilt of the sword. It's both so heavy it feels like it drags at me and so normal now that it feels like I've always carried it. "And his very clever maps. Without him, I wouldn't have found dear Duke Stekkan again, and I should honor that, don't you think Ilsaletta?"

I think it's a rhetorical question until I realize she's waiting for an answer.

"You could marry me still and save yourself this brutality," the duke suggests through swollen lips, and I'm grudgingly impressed by his swagger. His voice is laced in charm like poisoned wine and he even manages a smile that verges on a leer despite one of his eyes being swollen completely shut.

Jendaya takes a step toward him and her smile deepens. She takes his chin between her fingers and I'm battling surprise that his tactic has worked when she laughs.

"Maybe I like the brutality. Maybe I don't want saving. People always think princesses need saving. It's both annoying and convenient. I wouldn't have even learned that Ilsaletta still lived, if she hadn't tried to save me. Isn't that right, Ilsaletta?" She turns back to me again. "You owe me an answer, daughter of the Admiral. Should I honor the priest?"

Careful here.

My words are immediate and bitter. "I don't care what you do with him."

I don't like being betrayed. It stings like saltwater in a wound. I don't care who knows it.

Jendaya releases the duke and draws the priest back out of the shadows again. He grips his maps in white-knuckled hands. So. He realizes what a fool he's been to trust her. But he's too late. He's already in her grasp. I should pity him, but mostly I'm frustrated. He should have read more history books.

You thought she needed saving. He thought she needed his loyalty. Good people are easy to use and manipulate because they expect good in others. It's a flaw.

I flinch at his thoughts. They are too accurate.

Jendaya's smile deepens and her tone is light. "Well, if you don't care and I don't care …"

I don't even see her knife until it's in the priest's throat. He chokes, hands clutching at a bubbling red throat.

I take a step forward, the breath hissing from my lungs but there's nothing to be done. Our eyes meet in horror just before his glaze over and he slumps to the ground.

I feel like I'm choking but I don't know what I'm choking on. I feel like I'm going to pass out.

Deep breaths. In and out. He was dead the moment he betrayed you. He just didn't know it yet. It's not your fault.

The princess's tone is grim now. "You're not a very bright girl, Ilsaletta, or you wouldn't be here. You'd be halfway to the next country. But even a girl like you must finally realize that I am earnest in my intent to have that sword and book back, and I am just as earnest in my assurance that I will kill your pretty duke if you won't comply. This thing that used to be a priest is my evidence of that earnestness. You understand?"

I've never felt such rage as I do now. The priest is too dead to feel betrayed. But I feel it for him, and it sinks into my bones like black mold. I want justice. I want tables turned and roles reversed.

Easy now. Don't let emotions cloud your judgment. You're missing things. The guards are crowding closer. They want to see a spectacle. They've left gaps in the perimeter.

"He's not my duke," I say – because it's true and also because I don't want him to suffer because of her hatred for me.

"Isn't he?" Jendaya asks, stepping lightly over the priest and nudging her knife against Stekkan's throat. He is very still. I can imagine him swallowing and the knife nicking his bobbing adam's apple.

Isn't he? Vargaard echoes.

Well, if he is, then he's my responsibility. Stekkan's gaze isn't on the princess and the knife. It's on me. He's counting on me to save him. We need a way out that includes him.

Then we need more spectacle to draw the guards in further from their posts. I need you to draw attention. At the right moment, I'll tell you when to strike. Will you trust me?

With my life.

Will he trust me? Even when I've brought him to this fight against his will? Even when I've forced his hand?

My soul is in your slender hands. My trust is strung on your necklace.

I take another step toward the fire.

"Yours or not, I think you'll trade the sword and the book for his life," Princess Jendaya says. "Whatever advantage they offer you can't be worth watching someone die over, can it?"

She nods a head and one of the guards holding the duke balls up a fist and hits him hard where the neck meets the shoulder. Stekkan slumps under the blow, breath whuffing through his bruised lips. His eyes still never leave my face. I couldn't betray him if I'd planned on it. It would be like betraying a puppy.

"You can have the book," I say carefully. "But the sword is mine."

The princess's eyes narrow. "Wrong answer."

She nods again and the second guard slugs the duke in the belly – not once but three times until he's bent over double, sucking in breaths and making little sucking pained sounds like he's falling apart.

Something inside me is shivering. My thoughts won't fit properly in my head. This has gone too far. I've let it go too far. I risk a glimpse at the ring of people around me – or whatever they are now that they're filled with the spirits of other people from the past.

They're the haunted. The husks. The corricles.

They're also enjoying this. They seem to feed off the pain Stekkan displays, their eyes widening and the corners of their mouths lifting.

I want to be ill.

"I think you've read that book," Jendaya says. "I think you've noted its little hints and mysteries and you think you can use it to stop me. Which is why I want that sword, too. Not just because it grants you inhuman speed – makes you so fast that we can't even see your blows – but because it is one of the seven keys to stopping everything I've worked for."

She thinks that Vargaard is just me with magical speed that makes me so fast she can't see me strike. She's giving me a lot of credit.

"And I don't plan to let it stop me again. Give me the sword. Take your pretty duke. Walk away. I can't make you a kinder offer than that."

I walk until I'm close enough to the bonfire that my shadow stretches out behind me all the way to the treeline. Every eye is on me – or on the sword I'm holding out in front of me like a brand. I don't want to give it up.

I'm an excellent warrior. Fast. Clever. I can kill a man a thousand different ways. But I'm not quick enough to kill them all before someone kills you. We need to negotiate.

"Send the duke to me or I'll throw the book in the fire," I say, boldly. I've read it. I think I know most of it. But what if she calls my bluff? Will I really burn it?

"You won't do that," Jendaya says. I can see her face so clearly in the flickering light.

"I have two things I must negotiate for," I say with care. I see every eye on me. I must make this dramatic. I must do this perfectly. And I know I can't. I'm only a girl who likes to read about other people having adventures. But I try anyway. "I need the duke and I need to walk away without you killing us. You've already shown you don't mind killing. I've taken you at your word. Now, take me at mine and I know I will burn this book if you don't send the duke across to me. And if you do, I'll set the book down here and start backing up."

"And the sword?" she asks. I think she's holding her breath when she's done. She presses her lips together like she's trying not to show how nervous she is. Just like me. Neither of us feels entirely comfortable under the eyes of all these adults. What are they thinking? Are they judging us for being too young? Too foolish? Do they know something we don't know?

"The sword I give you when we reach the treeline – unharmed," I say. "And if that doesn't happen, then you don't get it."

She wants them both and she wants them badly. I can tell by the way her eyes are locked on the sword and how she swallows like she's afraid she's making as big of a mistake as I am.

"What do you need of trinkets?" the general beside her asks. "Just take the Admiral's daughter captive and we'll use her to shift him to our side of things. It won't take much."

Jendaya makes a chopping motion and to my surprise, his

eyes drift to where her aqua unicorn is flickering in and out of existence and he really does stop talking.

"You'll put the book down?" she presses.

"The moment I have him back," I agree.

I hope I remember what was written in it. I hope I didn't miss anything. I hope I'm not being a fool.

I hold my breath as she decides, and when she does it's all at once. She nods to her men.

"Set him loose."

A knife flashes and Stekkan's bonds are cut. One of Jendaya's guard shoves him hard, forcing him to stumble toward me, narrowly avoiding the fire. His face is so swollen on one side that one of his eyes is nothing but a narrow sliver. He careens into me, nearly bowling me over.

Adjust your feet. Take the blow. Let them slide with it. There you are.

Thanks to Varaard's advice, I don't fall over, but my heart is in my throat. Stekkan clutches at me as if I'm his salvation. He's trying to speak, and I shake my head.

"Run to the treeline toward the river," I whisper to him.

I don't look at him. I don't shake him off. All my concentration is in keeping my blade up and pretending to be strong. I pull the book from my pocket with a twinge of regret. Only the bold ever win. I've read that so many times in my books but now that my moment is here, I don't feel like I can do it. I'm doubting myself. I'm uncertain that I can see this through.

Uncertain about what?

"The book," Princess Jendaya calls.

I lift it high. I hope Vargaard is ready.

I wish you would tell me what we are readying ourselves for.

I can feel his breath on my neck, but I know it's only my imagination. No matter. It's time.

"It's yours," I call and I throw the book.

Chapter Twenty-Three

I'm a girl who likes hot tea and books. I'm not gifted in the art of throwing. I don't have to be for the book to arc through the air and land exactly where I want it to – in the heart of the fire.

I see Jendaya's eyes start to widen, but I don't wait. I spin in place and run and Vargaard runs with me in my long shadow, right in front of me. I swear I can feel his warmth as I plunge through the darkness. I can certainly hear his stream of curses. He sounds like he wants to bring the entire wrath of heaven down on us.

Betrayal? Breaking your word? That was your plan?

You can only fight treachery with treachery. I dealt with her exactly as she meant to deal with me.

Scourges.

My eyes are blinded by the fire. I can't see. I don't want to trip and impale myself on my own sword before they adjust.

Wind wooshes by and Vargaard shoves me roughly to the side. I stumble.

Keep your feet!

I do. Barely.

I have a vague sense of someone running ahead of me. Stekkan. His gait is poor. He's too injured.

I can't worry about him. I've done all I can for him.

A scream rips through the air behind me like tearing cloth. Vargaard is defending my back against enemies I can't even see. This time, I'm certain I feel the brush of Vargaard against my back and legs and seat. It's like he's embracing me from behind. The distraction makes me stumble.

Keep your feet and run!

It's hard to run when I feel him pressed against me.

Your shadow here is narrower than an eyelash, my sweet morning star. And while you fight bravely for your nation, you fight a much more powerful opponent.

I feel him surge and it pushes me forward. I start to turn.

Don't look back!

There's a sensation of movement and a cry. Something snaps. I feel ill at the sound. A shove against my back sends me stumbling and my sword tip dips down. I barely have the ability to bring it up in time to keep from tripping over it.

And that's when the madness erupts. It's a blur of sensation and quick reaction and Vargaard's orders in my mind.

Left! Duck. Faster. That's right.

The cries are from all around. I'm converged on by figures in the dark.

Shouts behind us urge them on, the princess's voice slicing through all the rest as she demands that they seize me before the sword gets away.

Something hot sears the back of my leg and I stumble at the same moment that a body drops in my path. I know it's a body. Its head is gone.

My momentum is too powerful, and I trip over it, my breath caught in my throat. One hand jars painfully into the ground, my palm scored as I skid across it to break my fall but though the knuckles of my other hand are aching from the fall, I don't lose my grip on the hilt in my other hand. I don't dare let it go. I won't.

My breath is so loud in my ears that it masks the sounds around me.

I'm on my hands and knees. I flip over so I can see behind me and gasp as Vargaard looms over me, his blade flicking out to slash the throat of a grasping guard. The enemy almost had me. He falls in a terrible stuttering drop as I crabwalk backward over the ground. Vargaard spins over me, crouched like a mother eagle over her chicks. He is focus and passion. I feel the tension of it in my mind. His shadow blade darts out and catches a second guard and before I can gasp, he's stepped over me again, shifting his weight in a pivot that spins him in a flurry of shadow and violence as he turns the blade of a third warrior at the last second.

I'm stunned. He looks like he is dancing over me – a bird in a complicated mating ritual. But this is a ritual of death and as I am still trying to catch my breath and clear my thoughts, another pair of guards drop and the bodies around me are piling up, blocking his shadow.

Up, sweet mortal girl, get up and run.

I can do that.

I claw my way up and dash toward the trees. I shift my grip on the hilt of my sword so I'm holding it backhand, the blade behind me. I won't be using it. That's clear now. It would be like a child fighting a lion. It would do me no good to have a blade. My blade and my shield are Vargaard and I abandon all other hope as I flee.

The run to the river seems to take twice as long as the walk from it had. Time stretches into years between my shuddering gasps and the powerful pulse of my heart. And I am the feather. I float over it. I form no thoughts. I can't bear to think as men appear with colored smoke bubbling from their throats and are dispatched just as quickly.

I'm almost to the trees when the ambush happens. They leap out, blocking my path and I'm suddenly surrounded by a ring of men.

Not good.

It's the first time I've heard that from Vargaard and then I feel a shudder in my mind. I spin and see him stumble. The men behind me are right there. Not even a pace away. The sword of one of them carves into Vargaard's left arm and he barely manages to twist away and avoid the follow-up backhand blow.

I stumble backward and that pulls him with me, but I'm not fast enough. Three more men attack as one and Vargaard's serpent-like flicking blade can only turn two of theirs in time. The third sword slices through, slashing across his ribs.

I flip my sword around in my hands and to my utter surprise, I charge. I still can't believe I'm doing it even as I crash into he nearest guard, sword thrust out in front of me in what has to be the most awkward attack a person has ever made.

No. Flee. Vargaard's voice sounds like a gasp in my mind and it only makes me more furious. I want these enemies to feel how they've hurt him – how they've hurt me.

My sword pulses, giving off an eerie light that's more the absence of light than actual light. It cuts through my enemy's defense and though my strength is weak, when it hits him, he convulses, falling to the ground and shaking, curling in on himself. His screams rip through the air like and injured rabbit's.

And now you run. Please.

I gasp and run. How did it do that?

All that stored up pain. I don't like how faint his mental voice is. *I wondered where it would go.*

But shouldn't he know?

I have no memory of it.

I'm looking behind me as I run, but the enemies attacking us are stunned, staring at the man still shaking from my attack. I should have fought them all. I shouldn't have turned and fled. I should have –

I crash into something hard and try to spin but arms wrap around me. He came out of nowhere. He has me locked tightly in his grip, his teeth bared and eyes full of fury.

I struggle against his grip, panicked. His breath smells of garlic. His face is twisted in concentration.

There's no help from Vargaard. I can't see him, but I can hear his quick panting and the curses and cries of those he fights.

Scourges. Scourges. Scourges.

We're overwhelmed.

The blade is dragged from my hands. I shriek my despair.

My heart is pounding too quickly. It chokes me. I'm reaching, reaching, reaching but it's gone.

I've lost it.

No. no. no.

They're taking him from me. My Vargaard.

I batter my fists against the guard, and he doesn't even flinch.

Someone is joining us with a lantern in his hand. The light bounces across the face of my captor leaving him ghoulish.

"Stop struggling, you little brat," he says. But I can't stop. I won't stop.

I'm overwhelmed.

Vargaard's words are too much for me. He's… he's …

I feel him and it's like he's a flame winking out. There one moment and then gone. And I don't have the sword. I don't have a way to bring him back.

Hollow despair rips through me worse than anything I've felt before.

Someone is yelling about the sword and the guard turns me roughly in his arms so I can finally see everything.

I can't stop the jagged gasping sobs that are ripping through me. I know I'm in hysterics. I can't seem to stop.

The surviving guards are picking up their fallen comrades – all except the one with my sword. He has it over his head and he's running toward Princess Jendaya in triumph.

And I might as well be dead. I've lost Vargaard. I've lost the sword and the book and in a moment, they'll bring me to her and she'll slit my throat like she slit the priest's and for what?

For *what*?

I should have listened to Vargaard.

I shouldn't have tried to be a hero.

Bitter despair fills what's left of my broken heart. I jam my teeth together and force myself to get my breathing under control, but I can't stop the tears that blur my vision.

"You've been a lot of trouble, girl," the guard holding me mutters. He's the last one this far back. Everyone else is limping toward the princess to join the victory. "Maybe I'll ask her to give you to me as my prize."

I bite my lip against the thought. What have I done? Vargaard told me to flee and I didn't listen to him. I should have listened. I shouldn't have thought I knew better.

I –

There's a heavy sound like a log being split and suddenly the guard's hands fall from me and something grabs my arm. I open my mouth to scream and a hand clamps around it, spinning me.

Nakuraki

I am not afraid.

Although I should be.

I should be worried that I was shredded and she's among enemies. I should be worried that the sword is being separated from her.

But I know dawn is coming.

Salvation is at hand.

Chapter Twenty-Four

It's Stekkan holding me. He drops his hand from my mouth and I gasp. His eyes are wide and bright in the moonlight and he clutches a heavy oar in his hand. It's darkened along the edge side.

I bite down on the scream bubbling up in my throat.

"Come on, monster hunter," he whispers.

Stekkan? My salvation? It's unthinkable.

They haven't noticed us yet. They're too intent on the sword. And it's too dark here on the edge of the trees. I break into a run behind Stekkan as we race toward the babbling river.

But half of me wants to run in the other direction. Maybe it's time to take Vargaards's advice, an hour too late. Maybe I need to regroup and come back for him later.

I can smell the water and the rushes that grow along the bank. I don't hear sounds of pursuit, only the wind rushing around me and the sounds of our pounding feet.

And the hollowness inside me.

I want to turn around and go back. I want the sword. I want Vargaard. I feel hollow and useless and all the wounds in my body ache without the sword's dampening power.

We reach the hidden boat. Stekkan has readied it. He leaps into the stern and I push against the bow. It won't take much to launch it. The river is fast.

I leap into the bow with a gasp of pain – not from my wounds, though they hurt now like never before. I'm hurting on the inside. My heart is cleaving in two.

I've grown attached to Vargaard. Which is ridiculous. It hasn't even been two full days since I met him. But I've begun to trust him – no, I've relied on him. Counted on him. I've put all my faith in him and now the sword is gone and that meant he is gone and this feels worse than Jendaya having Stekkan and the priest in her power. Oh, it's so much worse.

I can see her in my mind's eye lifting the sword. I can see my beautiful Vargaard manifesting in her shadow. I can see her eyes glittering with excitement as she raises the blade and lays claim to her new shadow bodyguard.

And he'll be trapped there forced to defend her.

And I will be alone.

When I come for her, he'll be there between us, defending *her*. Protecting *her*.

And it's all my fault because he *told* me that this was a stupid thing to do. He tried to change my mind. He tried to kiss me for heaven's sake.

Something squeezes my heart and I find I cannot breathe. I hate myself for being so stupid. I hate myself for thinking I could be a hero.

I can't even see the glow of their fires anymore. All I can see is Stekkan in the stern of the ship – and I can barely see that. It's so dark here there's hardly any light at all. A cloud is over the moon.

I should be glad. It hides our escape. We'll be so far down this river in just a few minutes that they'll have no hope of catching us.

We're free.

But my heart is back there with the sword. I know that now. Now that I can feel the ache of where Vargaard used to be. I want to hear him in my mind telling me what to do, and scolding me, and guiding me.

I just want him back.

I'm sick with wanting.

We shoot down the river for hours under the dark clouds and through the swollen river. It's smooth and fast.

I work mindlessly to keep the bow of the boat from tangling in fallen trees or tangles of branches. I'm cold all over. My hands are numb. Spray coats my face, and arms, and hair, leaving me bedraggled and shivering.

And I don't care, because my heart is numb, too.

How could I fail to realize what he meant to me until he was gone?

We reach the sea while it is still dark. The river shoots us out into it. Stekkan can barely keep his eyes open. I can tell he's in pain. He hunches over his middle and coughs often.

I beach the boat along the shore and pull it up so it won't be sucked into the sea and then I help him stumble up the sand dunes to a place where the sea cliffs can shelter him from the wind. Despite the cold, he's asleep the moment he's still, his rasping breath even and slow.

I am not asleep.

There is glass in my chest where my heart used to be. It hurts when I breathe. I don't know what to do.

I stare at the horizon. I'm facing west, so I don't see the dawn, just see the first glimmers of gold reflected on the black waves before me.

I stumble out of the shelter of the rock and look out to sea. Somewhere out there, my father is with his ships. They need to know what has happened. The rest of the world needs to ready themselves.

And we're the only ones who can tell them.

In a few minutes, I will pull myself together and find a plan for that. But right now, I'm watching as my shadow appears long and drawn out before me in the cold light of early dawn.

I'll never look at a shadow again without wanting to cry.

I had someone so precious. And I lost him because I was a fool.

I'm crying again. My eyes ache from it. I wrap my arms around myself, trying to hold my heart together as I blink the tears away.

The shadow ripples and distorts as I see it through my tears.

I dash them aside, but the shadow is still rippling and rolling.

And up out of its depths, a figure flows – wavering in the dawn light, dark and furious.

He spins, looking for enemies and when there are none, his eyes meet mine and his lips part.

He closes the distance between us and leans down like a hawk snatching prey.

And I can't feel his kiss. I can't feel his touch – not with my skin. But the warmth that fills my heart and the sudden rightness of the world is better than any physical sensation.

I want to live in this moment forever.

I feel like I know him as his shadow form wraps around me, his shadow cheek sliding against mine and never touching.

You're alive. You're alive. You're alive.

He almost sings it in my mind.

"But I lost the sword," I gasp. "I lost you."

He tries to wipe away the tears spilling from my eyes and then laughs when he can't. I'm laughing, too, in the middle of my tears.

The dawn is warm on my face and the sand solid under my feet and my shadow is long.

It's the second dawn, he whispers in my mind, his rumbling voice full of awe. *I should have explained. I tried, but I was interrupted.*

I don't understand.

I came with you. I told you I'd live in your shadow. When I made my vows to you after you opened the box, I left the shadow of the sword for your shadow. But it takes until the second dawn for the shift to be complete.

"But you made me think that you were tied to the sword!" My head is spinning. "I thought Jendaya had you now."

He smiles. How can a shadow smile like the dawn?

What would you have done if I'd told you that I'd tied myself to you – closer than family? Closer than a husband?

I bite my lip. I probably would have panicked. Then. Now it feels far too good to be true. I reach for him and touch nothing and the sweet bitterness of it washes through me like the tide lapping up to my feet.

And now? He asks me.

I'm anything but panicked. I can breathe again without that pain seizing my chest. I can think clear thoughts. I can feel.

"I wish I could hold you," I whisper.

But I cannot become corporeal without violence.

"Then love me violently."

That, my sweet mortal girl, I will never do. For you are my treasure and it is my solemn purpose to keep you safe and treasured.

And how can I argue with that?

"Do you think we can find the other swords?" I ask him. "Do you think they can be used to bring Jendaya down?"

I don't know. But I know this. If you go looking, I will come with you.

And that is more than enough for now.

***

Read more of Islaletta and Vargaard's story in *Blade of Shadow.*
Coming soon.

Behind the Scenes:

USA Today bestselling author, Sarah K. L. Wilson loves happy endings, stories that push things just a little further than you expect, heroes who actually act heroic, selfless acts of bravery, and second chances. She writes young adult fantasy because fantasy is her home and apparently her internal monologue is stuck in the late teens.

Sarah would like to thank **Eugenia Kollia & Melissa Wright** for their incredible work in beta reading and proofreading this book. Without their big hearts and passion for stories, this book would not be the same.

Thanks also to the Noble Order of Female Fantasy Authors who keep her sane – sort of.

And for her beloved husband, Cale and sons Neville and Leif who are endlessly patient as she talks to them about bookish passions.

She hope that you'll join her newsletter and check out her other books.

www.sarahklwilson.com